MISGUIDED REVENGE

COVERED BY GRACE

Christian Fiction

MARILYN STRONG

Paperback ISBN: 978-1-7356048-3-1

E-Book ISBN: 978-1-7356048-4-8

Audio Book ISBN: 978-1-7356048-5-5

DEDICATION

This book is dedicated to my parents, Leroy and Sarah Strong, and my favorite sister, Carolyn Strong (aka Polly). I miss you so much. To my friends and family who continue to support and believe in me, thank you. You are the wind beneath my wings.

Acknowledgments

I acknowledge my family and friends for their unwavering support and an endless supply of ideas. Special thanks to my church family, gym family, and the dance community.

READY TO SAY GOODBYE

Grandma had to be ready in two hours to bury her 35-year-old daughter, Madison. Her baby was gone, and she had to go to that darn church and put her most personal emotions on exhibit. It would feel like being a zoo animal while a volcano of feelings was erupting inside her chest and head. She would not wish this pain on her worst enemy.

After a fresh shower, she put on a bath robe which was a Christmas gift from Madison. She was in a daze, walking around the house in circles wondering what to do next. It was an out-of-body experience. She was moving in slow motion watching herself from another room. She kept asking: how did my child feel before the car accident on I-94 mangled her beautiful body? How much pain did she feel before God took her? How long did she wait for someone to rescue her? Did she call out to her mother? Did she expect her mother to find her? "Oh, Maddie, I cannot hold your hand, but I will always hold you in my heart."

The phone had an eerie silence. She was glad people were being respectful. The house was as noiseless as death itself. It was her choice not to have any out-of-town relatives stay there. Too much drama! She didn't want to be bothered with gossip about other family members. She sure didn't want to be responsible for feeding and entertaining them. The out-of-towners wanted to go shopping like this was a mini vacation. She would be glad when all the pretending was over. She needed time to collect herself.

It was difficult, but she made peace with God for taking her little girl. She may not have understood why God did what He did or why He allowed certain things to happen, but she had learned to trust Him and to rest in the trust.

As she felt tears starting to well up, she decided to move faster so she could be ready on time.

"OK, get a grip on yourself girl; no more tears, get ready."

She masterfully applied her foundation after watching a few online tutorials. She selected a lipstick that would not come off when eating at the repast. She usually wore glossy plum but today wore a mat plum. Eyeshadow was always a pain. The MizLadieRee online makeup tutorials had great tips. It was a lot of work, but she finished the bronze waterproof eye shadow. Her reflection in the mirror was flawless, and yet she knew she was going to be emotional and far from flawless.

The last thing to apply was waterproof mascara.

The loud pounding on the front door took her by surprise. The mascara smudged from the lower eyelid and toward her nose as she turned her head. She tried to rub it off before answering the door. Now it looked like she had a black eye.

She mumbled while walking to the door. "Why didn't they ring the doorbell? What the heck! The Butler Funeral Home is too early. Maybe they are bringing the cake to the house. I don't understand why they are here and pounding on the door like the police when they are too early."

She opened the door to find two guns pointing at her face. She quickly raised her arms as seen in so many movies. One gun was held by a black officer who looked like a seasoned bodybuilder who lived in the gym. The other was an Asian officer who seemed to love donuts.

In a trembling voice, she asked, "What is going on, officers?"

The black officer responded, "I will ask the questions here, Ma'am. Now keep your hands up and walk out of the house slowly."

The other officer asked, "What happened to your eye?"

"Nothing."

"Come on, I can see the bruise."

She laughed, "I was putting on make-up and the pounding on my door scared me and then it smudged. Please, tell me what is going on. My daughter's funeral is in an hour. I am mentally and physically preparing myself."

Their demeanor changed and they told her to put her arms down.

Mr. Muscle man said, "We are aware of the funeral today and are sorry we have to intrude at this time."

The Asian officer took over. "We will get to the point; your former son-in-law has a criminal record and listed this as one of his addresses. We need to talk to him for several reasons. One reason is that we are investigating to see if he had anything to do with Madison's car accident."

She gasped. "What are you telling me?" She fell back and Mr. Bodybuilder caught her before she hit the porch floor.

"We know your daughter had ties to Drake. He has several warrants. We will respect your daughter's funeral service. If he is there, we won't arrest him inside the church."

She was shocked. "If that's not enough, what else do you think Drake did?"

"We are not at liberty to say. But if he shows up here, please give us a call. Ma'am, here is a search warrant. We are going to search your home now. Please, wait on the front porch. By the way, that is a beautiful robe."

She sat on the porch in quiet distress. "Why did they have to do this today?"

Her son Jacob drove up with his triplets. The three grandbabies were in their teens and were incredibly cute. He parked and started walking to the porch. She motioned for him to get back in the car. The most rambunctious granddaughter, Kimberly, opened the door and started walking briskly toward her. She told Jacob to put her back in the car. Jacob was confused. "Ma, why are the police here? Did they hit you in the eye? I will kick their…."

"No, calm down, I was putting on my makeup when they knocked, and it smudged. They are looking for Drake. He is in some kind of trouble with the law."

"Why do they think he is here?"

"Boy, I don't know?"

Her stress came out in silent tears.

Jacob became concerned. "Ma, don't cry."

"I will be alright. Today is a rough day anyway and all of this commotion is working on my one last good nerve. You go ahead and do what you need to do so you can make it to the funeral on time."

"Ma, if you tell me you're fine then I will go. I don't want to leave you alone with the police if you are in trouble."

"I am fine. I am not in trouble, but they will be if they don't get out of my house. Now, you get going."

"We are making a quick trip to pick up some girly things before the funeral. Are you sure you're OK? I will stay if you want me to, but you know the police are not my favorite people."

"I will see you at the funeral son. Kiss my grandkids for me."

Grandma waved at the kids in the car.

Jacob had been in a lot of trouble growing up. She was surprised he did not end up dead or in jail. He had many fights in school, outside of school, and wherever he went. He was cursing out the teachers, skipping school, and smoking before he was thirteen. He even tried to sell drugs. Once, he had been smoking dope, got high, and stole her car. He went joyriding, not in the street, but on everyone's lawn. The only thing that stopped him was a big tree. It broke her heart when Jacob had a fistfight with his sick father while he was going through chemo for the lung cancer that took his life.

That son of hers had been stopped by the police many times. She understood why the police were not his favorite people. Jacob had a beautiful dark complexion, long hair, and a beard. He wore one dangly cross earring. He was a big guy about six feet five and 250 pounds. To strangers, he looked intimating, which is probably why he was stopped. When he was sixteen, his father had *the talk* with him about being stopped by the police, either while walking or in a vehicle: *Do whatever is necessary so you can get back home. Keep your mouth closed, no smart-talking; answer yes sir, no sir; or yes Ma'am, no Ma'am; no sudden moves; cooperate; show your hands with your fingers spread apart. Even if you are innocent, don't resist, let them take you to the station and I will take care of it when I get there. Above all for God's sake, don't ever run. It does not matter if you are guilty or innocent, do not run.*

Having the triplets made Jacob think about his future. She was proud of the man he had become. He was her only child left on this earth.

There were police cars parked on both sides of the street to the corner.

The neighbors come out one by one. They sat on their porches, nodded, and waved. They thought Jacob was in trouble again. After about 15 minutes, the police came out. The neighbors went back in and peeked out of the curtains.

The Asian officer added base to his voice and said, "We need to ask you a few questions."

"Go ahead but make it quick."

"When was the last time you saw Drake?"

"I have not seen him since he married my daughter and moved her to California many years ago."

"When was the last time you talked to him?"

She became aggravated because she was not ready for the funeral. "It's been years."

The Asian officer took a deep breath and inflated his chest then stepped toward her in an attempt to intimidate her. "So, are you telling us that when your daughter died, you did not call her ex-husband to inform him?"

She counted to three to calm herself. "Yes, that is exactly what I am telling you. Why would I call him? My wish for him is that he rots in Hell. I will offer my assistance in getting him to Hell. He abused my baby girl. He took her away from her family. He became a mean and demanding devil. I was glad she finally left him." She took another deep breath and stepped back. "Now, I have to get ready. I am done answering your questions." She raised her voice "Am I clear?"

The Asian officer looked surprised; "Yes, you are clear. We will be in touch."

The black officer walked toward the stairs and turned around to ask. "Who was that driving the dark-colored SUV when we were in the house?"

"That was my son, Jacob."

"Does he know Drake?"

She had reached her limit of patience with the questions. "Of course, he knows Drake, he was married to his sister. That is enough, I'm finished answering questions. Now get off my property," she yelled, "Now!"

The neighbor's curtains opened wider when she yelled at the officer.

The Asian officer said, "I got the license plate number and will follow up."

She waved her hand as if to say "whatever." She went into the house and slammed the door.

The house was a mess; they were looking for something or someone. The sofa cushions were on the floor. They pulled out the dining room chairs and they were upside down. The towels and sheets from the linen closet were in the hall. They overturned the mattress. The content in the dresser drawers was on the floor. She checked her office. The papers were not disturbed, but the closet door was open. She tidied up the living room and dining room making them acceptable for the company that was sure to come by after the funeral. She knew the police had a job to do, but this was not the day. She could hear Madison saying "Ain't nobody got time for that." She smiled at the thought of her smart mouth.

Grandma allocated two hours to get dressed and apply makeup, but only had 30 minutes remaining. Her hands were shaking, and she was a nervous wreck. She lay across the bed to calm her nerves and said a prayer.

Dear Lord, I don't know what's going on with Drake,
but I want Madison's service to be representative
of her beautiful life.
I want to remember saying goodbye to her.
Please give me strength, peace, and clarity of mind.
Lord, you said you would be a present help in the time of trouble.
I need your help in this present time of my troubled mind.
Please steady my thoughts.
Lord, please guide my tongue and my actions.
I am so drained and need you to keep me lifted
so I can survive this day.
I want people to see you when they see me.
Give me strength please Lord. Amen.

Peace and calmness came over her like a cool mist on a scorching day. She felt relaxed and calm. She looked in the mirror at her pitiful makeup job, washed her face, and started over.

KEN/IVY

Ken realized Ivy was taking a long time in the bathroom. "Babe, hurry up or you will miss the funeral."

"I can be a little late, but I will talk to Madison's Mom, Mrs. Michelle, during the repast."

"Make sure you play nice. You need to get invited to her house. We've gone over the plan to steal this lady's identity for what Madison did to us. First, you do your part, and then I will do the rest."

"Yes Ken, I know the plan, we've discussed it a million times. Chill out and let me do my part."

Ivy was easily aggravated with Ken and wanted him to shut up so she could have some peace. His nagging and need for validation were wearing her down. She knew she is a great catch for any man but has been in this relationship for five years and feels stuck.

Ken continued to push her buttons. "Get it in gear girl. It does not take that long to get ready. I am glad you watched that online video from MizLadieRee. She will show you how you should look in makeup. Your hair is alright, it is so short you don't have to do anything to it."

Ivy bites her tongue and continues to get dressed. She knew if she responded it would result in an argument.

Ken was getting enjoyment out of seeing her flustered. He felt less than a man because he was fired. He was being passive-aggressive and took his feelings out on her. "Babe, that dress is too tight. Are you putting on weight? Those shoes don't match that dress and are too high; you will probably trip and fall."

"Ken, if you don't shut up…"

"If I don't shut up, then what? What are you going to do? I was trying to be a courteous boyfriend and help you get dressed. You don't appreciate anything. Don't forget to bring me a plate from the repast."

GRANDMA

There was another knock at Grandma's door, softer this time. She answered the door in her robe. The driver was smiling. She noticed the limo car door was open ready for her to get in.

Before the driver could speak, she said, "Well, son, you will have to wait another thirty minutes. I am not ready"

He replied, "No problem, take your time. I will contact the church and let them know we are running late."

"Now that's how you do things. It is called customer service."

She put on an elegant black dress purchased for this occasion. Two of her girlfriends took her shopping. They went to specialty shops. Nothing "zinged" her. They hit the department stores, to no avail. As the girlfriends thumbed through the racks, Grandma sat as they brought potential dresses to her. Still, nothing excited her. They decided to go to lunch and shop another day. On the way home, around the corner from her house, she noticed a dress in the window of a little store. Her friends told her, it was a consignment shop and probably didn't have anything that was her style. When they went in, Grandma asked if she could try on the dress in the window. As she zipped it, her heart felt light, and then she exhaled. She could feel it deep down in her soul; this was the way she wanted to look when saying goodbye to her daughter. It was perfect. It fit like a glove. It was not too tight, but it fits in all the right places for this senior citizen who was killing it in the silver shoe class at the gym. Her friends bought her a beautiful black hat. They said it was appropriate for the mother to wear a black hat with a lacy veil to cover her face. This was a mourning tradition of the Victorian Era. *I don't think so. I am not a hat-wearing mamma.*

She wore a white pearl necklace with earrings to match. Her natural salt and pepper hair was in an updo. The black heels she chose were not too high yet comfortable enough to wear all day. A dab of perfume and she was ready to go.

She didn't remember the ride to the church. Her husband died several years ago. He should have been in the car; however, she felt his presence. She closed her eyes, and leaned back, pretending to be resting on his welcoming chest. She imagined him wrapping his powerful and muscular arms around her, enveloping her with love and comfort. Oh, how she missed that man.

When the limousine arrived at the church, the driver kept the reporters away so she could join the family. The church security officers told the reporters they could enter the church but had to sit in the balcony. They were not allowed to talk to the family.

Her family was waiting in the vestibule so everyone could walk in together. The grandchildren ran and hugged her. Sometimes teens could be so standoffish, but not today. She needed their hugs. Their affection meant so much.

Kayla, the quiet one said, "Grandma, you look beautiful. I like your eye makeup." She remembered how she looked on the porch. Kimberly and Cameron, her other grandchildren, hung on to her for dear life. Maybe she was comforting them, or they were comforting her. It felt appropriate having them near.

Kimberly was closest to her aunt Madison. Her mother, Emily, told Grandma that Kimberly was taking the death extremely hard. Sometimes she saw Madison's fire in Kimberly's eyes. Lord knows Madison had her smart mouth and short temper. Kimberly was beautiful and was wearing her hair the way Madison wore hers; a feathered pageboy in the front with the sides and back cut very close.

Her brother, Roy, always had her back. He was a few years her senior and started to show signs of age. The doctors told him two years ago that he needed a hip replacement. His back was starting to bend but still thinks he was The Mack, a woman magnet. He was about 6 feet tall and had a gorgeous head of gray hair. He hugged her, pulled out a bottle of water, and winked. That was his way of telling her if she started to feel faint, he would be there. He faded back to the middle of the family procession with the aunts, cousins, nieces, nephews, and friends.

She had her son, Jacob, his wife Emily, and the three grandchildren holding her up and she was ready to say goodbye to her only daughter.

Madison was super organized. She had a pre-arrangement policy with the funeral home. She wrote her obituary and program. She even picked out and paid for the casket, and the flowers she wanted on the casket. She was so thoughtful. All they had to do was show up. As Madison requested, the choir didn't sing. Grandma wondered why Madison didn't want them to sing because she used to sing in the choir. Recorded music from her favorite artists played over the sound system.

Her baby girl looked like an angel. Her hair was just the way she was currently wearing it, but it had an extra shine, almost like a halo.

Her skin glowed. The funeral home used her makeup. When she was alive and smiled that full-faced smile, you could see her dimples. In the casket, Grandma saw her dimples. Her baby was smiling when she met her maker. Madison enjoyed wearing lipstick. If she didn't wear any makeup, she would wear her trademark lipstick. The shade was perfect. She was beautiful. The funeral home asked for her favorite perfume. When she kissed Madison, it was comforting to whiff the aroma of her perfume. She was dressed in a beautiful white dress. The sequences caught the light, and she was a sparkling diamond. Her mind kept flashing images: the tiny little girl, the teenager who was bold and sassy and knew everything, her first heartbreak, and the young executive working for Ford Motor Company. She saw them in the casket. She was ready to say goodbye to them all.

It was a nice service. As anticipated, she cried and whaled like a baby. When it was time to close the casket, the funeral home honored her special request. To avoid people crowding around trying to get the last view while Grandma was trying to close the casket, she asked the funeral home to roll the casket over to where they were sitting. This kept the crowd back and forced them to give her the moment.

Grandma stood up and kissed her girl goodbye. She immaculately folded the delicate satin fabric into the casket. She tucked her in just like when she was a child. This was her last *mommy-and-me* moment. The funeral home let her assist in the slow closing of the lid. Hearing the clunk when it closed startled her. She got weak in the knees and dropped down on the church pew. Roy pushed everyone out of the way to get to his sister. He sat with her to make sure she was alright. The pastor asked the nurses to assist her. After a few minutes, she told Roy that she was feeling better. He left and went back to his seat. They rolled the casket back to the original spot. The rest of the service was a blur. She didn't remember a thing the pastor said, the remarks from her friends, the condolences, or any of the songs. Closing the casket lid was more draining than expected.

The church provided a complimentary video or audio recording. Grandma selected the video because she knew she wouldn't remember everything about the service. The funeral home gave its signature speech. "We would like to give you this cake because we know it's hard to feel sad when you are eating cake." That always got a laugh out of everyone.

THE REPAST

Since Madison wanted to be cremated, everyone went to the church basement for the repast immediately after the service. Her friend, Deborah, put together a bittersweet slide show. There were such beautiful pictures of Madison having fun. She knew a lot of people and some who were in the slide show were also at the funeral and repast.

Jacob was in the corner talking on his new phone. "Drake, you have to stop calling me. I am at my sister's funeral."

"I know that, and I am so sorry I can't come to the funeral and speak to your mother. I calling to make sure you are still down with the plan and your emotions are in check."

"Man, get off of my phone. No, my emotions are not in check, I am at my sister's funeral. Yes, I am still going through with the plan. After we are done, I don't ever want to hear from you again." Jacob hung up the phone.

Jacob was trying to stay low because he didn't want his family to know he was planning illegal activity with Drake. They had been talking for months.

Between eating and accepting condolences, a young woman about Madison's age approached Grandma.

"Hi Mrs. Michelle, I was friends with Madison. We worked together for a short time. I want to introduce myself and would like to keep in touch with you."

She remembered seeing her face but could not place where they met. She was so sweet and attentive. They talked for about fifteen minutes. Grandma thought she said her name was Ivy. They exchanged phone numbers. Ivy had on a wedding ring but was not accompanied by her husband. She went on and on about how she and her husband esteemed Madison and how Grandma raised a beautiful person. She mentioned that she was also at the funeral of her husband and that they spoke briefly at his repast at her home. For the life of her, Grandma couldn't remember Ivy or her husband.

The conversation with Ivy was interrupted by loud bellowing and screaming of someone entering the church basement.

Wait a minute. No, not my sister. She was Madison's birth mother. *How could she show up, with her trifling, drunk, crackhead butt? She is wearing dirty blue jeans, a torn tee shirt, and muddy gym shoes. Her hair was matted locks. She had the nerve to have on a black hat with a lacy veil like she is the mother who raised Madison. I should snatch that hat off of her head and stuff it down her throat. She missed the entire service. Did she come for the free food?*

Grandma motioned to one of her church members, "Keep her away from me."

But no… her sister had to get in her face. She whaled between tears, "My daughter is dead. It is your fault. I never should have let you raise my daughter. Stand up hoe, so I can kick your butt in this church. I mean it, I will kill you right here and we can have two funerals today."

Grandma kept her peace because a wise lady told her, "Don't ever argue with a fool because someone watching won't be able to detect the real fool."

Their brother Roy stood in front of Grandma and dared their sister to come close. Roy said in a stern steel voice, "Don't let your mouth write a check your ass can't cash." Then he motioned to the deacons, "Get that dope fiend out of here."

Finally, the church security team escorted her out. The family surrounded Grandma. More hugs from the grandkids. The church gossiping click huddled in a corner. This should keep them talking for a while.

Her only sister could perform like she was so hurt, but she was dead to Grandma. When Madison was about six, she allowed her to be sexually assaulted by her no-good boyfriend. Then she beat Madison until blood was running down her back. That same day, she kicked her out of the house. She gave Madison to Grandma to raise. She and her husband were overjoyed when the adoption was final, and Madison was legally their daughter.

There were so many people in the church basement at the repast. She was glad the reporters were not allowed in this space. She spotted the undercover police in the corner. They couldn't hide. This was Detroit, we can smell them. Luckily, Drake didn't show up. They didn't need any more drama.

She socialized and chatted with friends. There were lots of pictures taken after the meal. There were many posts on social media. Who knows the next time all of them will be together again, so they took advantage of the photo opportunities. The grandchildren savored the attention. Grandma stayed a little longer and talked with more of Madison's co-workers.

FUR BABY/GRANDMA

Grandma's son, Jacob, drove her home from the service. She was carrying the cake, the sign-in book, the sympathy cards, and the thank you for attending cards. The grandchildren were talking in the back seat. She cherished the time while listening to them. She would ear hustle to keep up with what was going on in their lives.

She gave her brother, Roy, the key to the house, knowing he was not going to stick around and chit-chat. She asked him to open the door for the family. When Grandma arrived, there was a tiny army already there. She was glad she had tidied up after the police. The church sent over the excess food. Everyone was taking pictures, eating, and enjoying each other's company.

She noticed that her dog, Olivia, was not in the room. Olivia was a cute little Yorkie Grandma rescued. One day two huge dogs were chasing her, and Olivia ran on her porch. She was nasty and smelled very bad. When the big dogs saw Grandma, they ran away. She sang a song and Olivia allowed petting on her head. Olivia was hungry, so she gave her part of her ham sandwich and a bowl of water. She took Olivia to Animal Control to see if she had a chip, but she did not. She visited Olivia every day at Animal Control Center. She would sing to her and her ears would perk up. Since the owner did not claim her within the specified time, she took Olivia home. She was not a yapping dog. She seldom barked, but when she did, she sounded like a big dog. Somehow, she learned to disguise her bark to make the other dogs think she was tough. It took Olivia a while to understand she didn't have to hide her food. She didn't know she could sleep in a dog bed and not on the floor. After a few weeks, she gained Grandma's trust. They were like two peas in a pod. Grandma put her in an oversized purse, and they went everywhere. Olivia had a peaceful spirit and lived to cuddle.

After greeting the family inside the house, she checked outside because Olivia goes through the doggy door to do her business. She was on the ground wining and yelping for help in a frail voice. She was in distress. One of the guests heard Grandma scream, went outside, and brought Olivia into the house. She looked and sounded bad. Olivia never followed her in the kitchen, but now she was limping behind her every step. After a few hours with her guests, Grandma noticed Olivia was not getting better. Jacob drove Grandma and Olivia to the emergency veterinarian across town. Driving took forever. I-94 was full of potholes, but I-75 was a little better. They took an exit to a narrow street without streetlights and was pitch black. She almost had heart failure because Jacob was driving so fast.

The vet saw them immediately and assessed her destitute condition.

She asked, "What is wrong with her?"

The vet replied, "Ma'am, she fell. She has a broken tailbone and a broken jawbone. She is so fragile that she would not survive the surgery. At her advanced age, the kindest thing to do is to let her go."

They vet took them to a private room. Grandma talked to Olivia while rocking her to comfort her during her last minutes alive. Then she started singing and sobbing at the same time. Olivia was resting in her arms in pain but at peace, because she trusted Grandma's loving arms. The nurse came in and put an injection in her arm. She told her that Olivia's eyes would remain open when she passed. Grandma held the sweet fur baby companion that had been at her side for a decade. She felt the life leave Olivia's body as her dog took her last breath. The staff was so kind in letting Grandma stay with Olivia as long as she wanted. She cried so much that when she left there was a puddle on the floor. She saw them bring in a mop and bucket when she was filling out the paperwork.

The ride home was nauseating. Grandma was drained and felt terrible. Her head was throbbing on the right side. It felt and sounded like there was a jackhammer inside her skull. Her vision started to blur, and she could hardly breathe.

She tapped Jacob, "Son, I don't feel well. My head is killing me." She tried to explain what she was feeling.

He looked at her and immediately drove her to the Hospital Emergency Room. Jacob was nervous and had never seen his mother look so bad. Thank God they were close to home, and he knew where the hospital was located. He parked the car and told her to wait inside the car. She was very fragile. He got a wheelchair. Jacob never assisted anyone in getting into a wheelchair. He didn't know how to lock the wheels, and the wheelchair kept moving backward. He didn't know to lift the footrest so she could put her legs in easily while sitting down in the chair. He helped her get back into the car. He went inside the hospital and asked one of the nurses to come out and assisted him. They wheeled her in, and she was seen immediately.

Her blood pressure was 200/100. The medical staff was running, darting in and out of the room. They put her on a gurney and wheeled her into what looked like an operating room to take tests. They asked her the standard questions: Who is the President of the United States? Do you know where you are? What day is it? What month is it? What medications did you take today? When she came back to the emergency room waiting area, her brother, Roy, was there with Jacob. The nurse gave her more medication and asked her to stay awake. They took her blood pressure every fifteen minutes. The doctor came in to give his assessment. While they were running tests, Jacob told the doctors about the events of the day.

The doctor simply said, "You've had a stressful day. Your body's response was normal. You should see your primary doctor soon."

When Roy saw that they were not keeping her, he said his goodbyes. After they completed the paperwork, they put Grandma in a wheelchair and rolled her to the car.

Jacob wanted them to keep her in the hospital overnight for observation. "Ma, you scared me. I'm glad you are not dying. I thought I was going to lose you too."

"I'm glad I'm not dying too. This was a very difficult day. My body needs some rest."

When they arrived at the house, a few family members remained. She said hello and goodnight in the same breath, then went straight to bed. She didn't have the energy to answer questions, listen to stories or be sociable while her heart was aching for her daughter and her fur baby. Roy explained to everyone what happened with Olivia and the tests at the hospital. He asked them to leave so she could get some rest. Roy set the burglar alarm, locked up the house, and left.

Grandma got dressed for bed and reflected a little bit. *What a day! I Said farewell to my only daughter and my fur baby companion on the same day. I have never gone through so much in one day. I had to confront my good-for-nothing sister. The devil is busy. My God, how did I survive this day? I am drained. Why did all of this happen to me on the day I said goodbye to Madison? I cried a river today.*

As usual, she got on her knees for her nightly prayer.

Dear Heavenly Father, this has been a horrific day.

My God, I miss my daughter.

There is a hole in my chest that is indescribable.

It is finally hitting me that I will never see my child.

I feel like my entire chest is caving in and I am too weak to stop it.

A parent should never have to bury a child.

I fear I will never be the same.

God, I ask you to help me to bear this load.

Lord, I know my fur baby, Olivia, has crossed the Rainbow Bridge.

I miss her and the sound of her paws running through the house.

God, please help me deal with the loneliness and pain.

Help me accept my new normal.

God, I know that earth has no sorrow that heaven cannot heal.

I am trusting and believing in you to restore me.

In your son Jesus' name I pray, Amen.

NO CHURCH SUNDAY

Grandma didn't want to be sad or distressed. She turned on the Smooth Jazz radio station. A long bath would relax her and center her emotions. She put a little Epsom salt in the water to relax the tight muscles and lavender oil for aroma therapy. On the bath tray, she had a tall glass of cool orange juice, grapes, and a romance novel. She soaked in the warn bath, sipping orange juice and reading while letting her mind drift. She was so relaxed. She put the book down and floated on the music. A song came on by the saxophonist, Duane Parham. *Oh, my goodness*, she thought, he was making that horn talk to her. *He is so smooth.* Music had a way of helping her release anxiety and stress. Usually, Olivia was on the rug in the bathroom while she was soaking. She missed her. She had to accept the enormous changes in her life and go through the grieving process then move forward. But she knew the grieving process did not follow the printed pages. She could be in stage one in the morning and stage five in the afternoon. Now, she wanted to relax and disappear from everything in this nice bath and great music.

The phone rang. *Who is this disturbing my peace?* The caller ID said, Jacob. "I am not going to answer it." He was persistent. Jacob called back twice.

In an annoyed voice, she answered, "Hello."

"Ma, how are you doing?"

"I am doing ok, what about you?"

"You went through a lot yesterday. I know you miss Olivia running around the house. Do you want some company?

"No son, I need to relax and not think about anything."

"Make sure your doors are locked and be careful when you go outside."

"I am always careful. Why are you telling me this? What are you talking about, son?"

"I think Drake is in Detroit."

She turned off the radio, pushed the tray forward, and sat up in her bathwater. "What, when, where?"

Jacob nervously answers, "I can't tell you how I know."

"Boy, if I had not heard you say that I would not have believed it myself. Do you know how he treated your sister? You better not have that animal at your house and around my grandkids. If the police don't kill you, I will."

"No Ma, it's not like that. He had some business in Detroit and came by to say hi. He wanted to see you too, but I told him not to go to your house. He has some kind of breathing problem."

"Son, there is no way on God's green Earth I want to ever see Drake. Anyway, do you know the police think he had something to do with Madison's accident?" Grandma closed her eyes in an attempt to remain calm. "I don't want to think about that now. I am relaxing and trying to keep my blood pressure down."

There was a knock at the door. "Who is that at my door now?" She mused, still on the phone. "It's probably the neighborhood meth head. I give him the soda bottles so he can cash them."

Jacob yelled, "Ma, don't open your door."

"Son, I will look out of the window first, and then open the door. I need to get a camera doorbell so I can see who is out there. Wait, now they are pounding on my bedroom window. That's not the meth head. I am getting my 45. If it is Drake, I will shoot him and drag him into the house. Get over here, son. I am going to call 911 now."

"I am on my way."

She hung up the phone and started to call 911. The phone rang again.

She answered and yelled, "Jacob, stop calling me."

A timid voice replies, "Hello, Ma'am this is Ivy, I was just checking on you."

Annoyed, she responded, "Baby, this is not the time," and hung up the phone.

The knocks on the bedroom window were getting louder. She dialed 911 again, but before she could finish the phone rang again.

"Jacob, is this you again?"

"Hello, this is Medicare and you qualify for a free knee brace."

She yelled on the phone. "Man, if you don't get off my phone. I am about to have my house broken into and you are talking about a darn knee brace."

She jumped out of the tub and put on her robe. She retrieved the gun from the safe and put it in her pocket. She heard police sirens and loud pounding on the door. She peeked through the curtain and saw the same two police officers who were there yesterday. She hid the .45 in a little cubby box near the front door, tightened her robe, and opened the door.

"What is going on, officers?"

The black bodybuilder officer responded. "We hate to bother you again, but we got a report that Drake has been spotted in this neighborhood. Are you alright?"

"Yes, I am fine. Why? Do you think Drake is going to hurt me?"

"Ma'am, we don't think he will hurt you, but maybe he will contact you for a place to hide out."

"Trust me, officer, if he comes here, I will bust a cap in his butt. There is no love between us."

The Asian officer said, "We have the neighborhood staked out with unmarked cars. If he is near, we will get him."

Jacob arrived minutes after the police left. She scolded him; "If I was in danger, I would be dead. What took you so long to get here? It was the police pounding on my door and window. They are trying to serve warrants on Drake. Now you listen and listen well. If you are planning on seeing that monster, don't do it. Don't even go where you think he might be because when, not if, but when the police arrest him, they are taking everyone with him. Madison told me he has operations set up in different parts of California and he distributes drugs in Mexico, Arizona, and California. He is manufacturing meth and making opioids. He puts fentanyl in everything, which was his trademark. This guy does it all, the young guys call him the Godfather. He was always strapped with multiple guns. Madison told me everything after she left him. She was always afraid that he would come after her because she knew too much. When she found out about his criminal activity it frightened her and she came back to Detroit."

"Ma, she told me that stuff too. I thought she was making it up as an excuse to leave him. Anyway, I am not dealing with Drake. Since you are OK, I will see you later."

That ended her relaxing time. She made breakfast and started her day.

DONATING MADISON'S CLOTHES

It was an emotional and physical chore sorting and donating Madison's clothes. Canceling her cards and automatic monthly bank deductions was difficult because Grandma was asked to explain the death over and over. The most insensitive was the monthly car wash company. Madison had a plan where she paid once a month and got as many car washes as desired. This company kept dipping into the bank account even after the death certificate was mailed. After most of the debts were settled, Grandma closed the account. That darn car wash company sent invoices to the house for back payment.

Madison had stocks, bonds, a 401K and three different life insurance policies. She had an attorney file a trust, and all of her assets were owned by the trust. Grandma was the executor so they didn't have to go through probate. While going through Madison's papers, she came across a canceled Certificate of Deposit. It appeared she did not collect the interest. She remembered her boyfriend Ken worked in the securities exchange. He probably talked her into getting it. She wondered why it was canceled.

As her mother, Grandma kept precious memories to preserve the spirit of her little girl. She sealed Madison's favorite dress in a waterproof garment bag. When the pain of missing her got too great to bear, she unzipped the bag, hugged it, and got a whiff of Madison.

She asked Jacob to bring the triplets and their mother, Emily, to get keepsakes.

Kimberly was always the first to respond, "Grandma, I want to remember Aunt Madison forever. I miss talking to her."

"Yes baby, I miss her too. So, I want each of you to take anything of hers so you can have a piece of something precious to her."

They selected items to remember their Aunt. Kayla and Kimberly wanted her jewelry and a few pair of shoes. Cameron took a picture she purchased in California of the Santa Monica Pier. Her brother Roy only wanted a miniature ceramic statue. Her loyal friend, Deborah, picked out a cute dress. Jacob took a ring that he put on a chain and wore around his neck.

Grandma contracted an estate planning agency to organize an estate sale. It was advertised in the local paper. She went to the sale, but it was difficult watching people pick through the stuff. The estate planning agency kept a 40% commission. They didn't make a lot of money on Madison's stuff, but most of the items were gone. It was time to donate what didn't sell and then put the house on the market. Grandma's brother, son, and grandson rented a U-Haul and dropped off the remaining items at *Interfaith Works*. This agency helped people who were homeless and living in poverty. Unlike other organizations, Interfaith Works didn't charge for the items, they give away everything. This was what Madison would have wanted. Her beautiful house sold in one week.

JACOB/THE 5-SIR COMPANY

Jacob finished truck driving school with honors. He was certified to drive 18-wheelers. Emily drove everyone to the graduation ceremony. Grandma was so proud of her son. He finally completed something. Lord knows they had their disagreements about him keeping a job. With Madison gone, he felt the need to step up to the plate and be the man he was raised to be.

After the graduation ceremony, the family went for Ice cream. Grandma was chatting with the grandchildren, Kayla and Cameron. Kimberly usually was the most talkative, but today she seemed withdrawn. They talked about school and their projects. Kayla teased Cameron about the girls liking him. Oh, these kids were her heartbeat. She remembered a joke told by a minister, "If I knew grandkids were so much fun, I would have had them first." She understood very well what he was talking about. They were such a delight.

She wanted to pull Kimberly into the conversation. "Kimberly, you are kind of quiet, is everything OK?"

She snapped back. "Why are you asking me that? Did you ask Kayla and Cameron if they were OK? Grandma, why are you picking on me?"

She was shocked and clapped back. "Now wait a minute young lady. First of all, you never speak to me in that tone. And secondly, I can ask you whatever I want to ask, whenever I want to ask, and I expect an answer. Am I clear?"

Immediately her mother, Emily, came over. "Grandma, let's take a walk."

She had a feeling there was more to Kimberly's response.

Emily began, "I apologize for how rude Kimberly is being. I'm not making excuses, but she started her period a few months ago and we are trying to figure out those raging hormones. One minute she is as sweet as pie, the next minute she is bawling her eyes out. Some days she is in a fetal position in a corner rocking. And the worst is when she is loud, vulgar, and disrespectful. She called me a bitch and a whore; she slams doors and stomps off when I try to talk to her. It's almost like she is possessed."

She had Grandma's full attention. "She is a late bloomer. I started when I was fourteen. Have you talked to her about the mood swings and let her know this is expected? Is she prepared to handle this? What about Kayla, has she started yet?"

"Yes, Kayla started a month before Kimberly, and she does not seem to be affected by the mood swings. Kayla and I tried talking to Kimberly, but it was like pulling teeth, or it became a shouting match."

"Emily, we had to go through the teen years. I had a lot of attitude. When I think about how mean I was to my mother, I'm surprised she didn't kill me. We will get through this with Kimberly." They walked back to the bench where the rest of the family was sitting.

Kimberly ran to meet her, with a big hug and sorrowful eyes. "I'm sorry, Grandma."

Grandma was touched. "Kimberly, you are going to have days where your emotions are all over the map. It will be difficult, but you can control yourself. Those crazy feelings and thoughts won't last forever. Baby, this attitude of yours doesn't make sense. When you feel a boiling rage and are about to say or do something, know that you are feeling anxious and off-balance. Before your respond or act, it's a nice idea to say a quick prayer. Just ask God to help you. Once I asked God to help me, so I didn't kill this fast-talking salesperson trying to take advantage of me."

Kimberly laughed, "Thank you, Grandma. You always make me feel better. Can I come to your house tomorrow after school?"

"Sure, clear it with your parents first."

KIMBERLY/GRANDMA

After school, Kimberly was at the door. Grandma was not sure which personality she was about to experience. Luckily, it was the sweet little Kimberly.

They went to the kitchen to talk around the table. Together, they prepared her favorite snack, grilled cheese, and tomato soup. After their snack, the floodgates of conversation started.

Kimberly began to open up, "Grandma, sometimes I hate myself and don't know why. I feel hopeless. When people look at me, they are looking through me and I am invisible to everyone unless I am with Kayla and Cameron. Sometimes I start talking loud so people will see me."

Grandma held her tongue while Kimberly emptied her heart. "There is a boy who picks on me at school. I think he likes me, but his words make me feel bad. He calls me silly names and then says he was just joking and that I can't take a joke. But it feels like he is giving me a backhanded compliment and insulting me at the same time. I have a teacher who never acknowledges my hand when I raise it because I know the answer but calls on me when I don't raise my hand. I feel stupid because I don't know the answer and the kids laugh at me. I can't concentrate in school because every time the door opens or I hear a loud sound, I think a gunman is coming into the school to shoot everyone. Sometimes I wish someone would kill me because that would stop these feelings. I hate going to school. All of my friends are on social media and are having so much fun and I feel down in the dumps. My mother hates me. A little voice keeps telling me to off myself because no one loves me, and everyone would have a better life if I was not around because I am such a downer. I hate myself."

Grandma tried not to show her true feelings. She thought, *No, not ending your life, baby no.* But she didn't interrupt while Kimberly was on a roll.

Kimberly took a deep breath and continued, "When Aunt Madison was alive, we talked a lot. She would listen and always knew what to say to help me. I know mom and dad try their best, but they don't know anything. I came to you because I trust you. Old people know stuff and can get a prayer to God. Grandma, I know I need help. I am hurting inside. Can you help me? I don't know what to do, or what to feel. Tell me what to do when I feel like this. I feel so useless?" She started to blubber uncontrollably.

Grandma's wisdom recognized that the emotions were out of control. Answering her questions now would not be fruitful. She hugged Kimberly, sat back in her chair, and held her hand as she continued.

"Please don't tell my parents what I told you. I trust you. Mom and Dad don't get me, they want to yell at me or punish me."

She was shaking like a leaf. It cut Grandma to the core of her being to hear her grandchild talk like that.

She grabbed her precious grandchild and held her tight; rocking her like she was a baby while silently asking God to give her the right things to say. Fighting back her tears while holding her, she started to pray.

My Dear Jesus, please hear our prayer.

My grandchild is in so much pain.

Dear Lord when these thoughts and negative feelings come to her,

I ask you to open her heart so she can feel your love.

I ask you to open her ears so she can hear your words.

Please calm her thoughts and the noise

in her mind so she can hear you.

Let her feel your love like a strong gentle wind,

let that love settle her mind and calm her fears.

Remind her of the 91ˢᵗ Psalm. That you will always protect her

and is with her at all times.

Let her know that you see and understand her

struggles and that she is not alone.

Strengthen her mind. Give her self-confidence and self-esteem.

Dear Lord, remind her of the crown she wears

and that she is a queen and your child.

Dear Lord, protect my baby.

Father, please bring the scriptures

to her mind that she has been raised with.

Let her know that she is a conquer.

Help her to tell the anxious feelings to go away

and allow your Holy Spirit to take over her mood

to calm and relax her mind.

Thank you, Lord. In your son Jesus' name we do pray, Amen."

Kimberly stopped trembling and her face was more relaxed and peaceful. Tears of sorrow were now tears of calm peace. Kimberly hugged Grandma tighter, went to the bathroom, and washed her face. There was a shift in her energy. She walked with peaceful confidence. She gathered her things while heading to the door.

Before Kimberly left Grandma had to give her a scripture. "Kimberly, the tongue is a tiny part of your body, but it can be evil and full of deadly poison. You have to control it. When you get home, open your Bible to the Old Testament. Go to the book of Proverbs. Next, go to the sixteenth chapter and read the thirty-second verse. It says. *"He that is slow to anger is better than the mighty, and he that ruleth his spirit is better than he that taketh a city."* Honey, remember to rule your emotions, and not let your emotions rule you. You don't need to be extra or tough. Saying the wrong thing at the wrong time and the wrong way can affect your outcome in life. Slow down that anger. Baby, you are loved. Control yourself and watch how things will fall into place."

"Thanks, Grandma. See you at the first Sunday Dinner."

JACOB/GRANDMA/CAMERON

A week after his graduation, Jacob called Grandma with the great news that he had gotten a job driving for the 5-Sir Company. The drawback was that he would be out of town more than he was in town. Meanwhile, her grandson Cameron had discovered he can do more than pee "with it." He needed that *father-and-son* chat. These girls were chasing him, and he was letting them catch him. Once he had a crush on Sha who was her friend Sandra's granddaughter. Sha was older than Cameron, but he still tried to talk to her. She was beautiful, very streetwise, and money hungry. She would talk to Cameron and lead him on. Once she asked him to take her on a date. Since he didn't work, he had to save his allowance and he still didn't have enough to take her out. She dressed provocatively. She was seen at the fruit market wearing a tight crop top with more breasts out than in. She had on booty shorts with cut-outs on the side and her butt checks hanging out. She was advertising and there were a lot of men answering the ad. Sha was bad news.

One day, Cameron showed up at Grandma's house unannounced. He was panting, "Grandma I need to talk to you."

She was surprised, "OK, baby, get in here."

He paced around for a little while, got an apple out of the refrigerator, and began to talk.

"I have a feeling that someone is always following me, so I decided to run a little. There is this girl named Bella, and she likes me, and I like her a lot."

She interrupted. "I know you are not talking to those fast girls like Sha. Is Bella the girl you brought to Sunday dinner a few months ago?"

He was aggravated. "No Grandma not her, just listen. When I met her at the mall, my gut said not to talk to her, but she needed my help. She was so beautiful. She is shy and does not talk much, but I like her. I get butterflies in my stomach every time we are together. Grandma, what troubles me is that some girls in my school said Bella has been threatening them if they try to talk to me. This does not sound like the Bella I know. I think they are jealous of her."

"What do your sisters think of her?"

He looked surprised. "I haven't told them."

"Now be truthful with me boy, have you received naked pictures from this girl?"

He looked shameful. "Grandma, how do you know stuff like that? No, I told you, she is very shy and quiet."

"Tell your sisters, they may know more about her. You know girls talk."

"But we go to different schools, they probably don't know her."

"Baby, trust your gut. If your gut says something is not right with her, you might have to let her go. If you break up with her, be a gentleman. Be kind but firm. Let her know it is over and there is no way it will work. Ignore any attempts to get your attention. Ignore texts, emails, or any kind of flirting or temper tantrum. If she is a stalker or is threatening folks, your safety is my main concern. Keep your distance from her. Try not to be alone with her. If you can't block her on social media or make it private, you might need to get another account. Change your routine, going to and from school, or hanging out with friends and stuff like that. Start a journal writing every day and we might have to take it to the police. Keep my words in the back of your mind. Cameron, it would be a lovely idea if you prayed before you got involved with these girls. Always listen to and obey your gut feelings. But baby, if she turns out to be as sweet as you say, then just roll with it."

"Thanks, Grandma, that sounds like a plan. But one more thing, I had a dream the other night. I was half awake and half asleep. I heard what sounded like a herd of dogs coming down the hallway. My room filled up with enormous creatures. The ringleader had a colossal alligator head and dog hoofs. He was standing on two legs. He kept bobbing his head up and down while looking at me. There was a very foul smell. First, he sat at the end of the bed. Then he got in bed with me, and I couldn't move. I didn't feel it touching me. I was so scared. I couldn't scream. All I could do was blink my eyes. Grandma, I know it was Satan. Finally, I was able to speak, and I said Jesus, Jesus. And all of them went away. I lay there and wondered what happened. The next morning when I asked my sisters if they heard anything strange sounds like dogs walking in the house, they thought I was crazy and said they didn't hear anything."

"That was a terrible experience. You did the right thing because the evil one knows the name of Jesus. I believe you were visited by Satan and his fallen angels. You have to keep praying and reading your Bible. Stay close to God. You can't fight the spirit of Satan all by yourself. You need God. You have a gift and Satan knows it. He is trying to scare and distract you. Hold on, be avid and of good courage. If something like that happens again, and you are unable to talk, do what you did, and keep repeating the name of Jesus. Also, repeat in your mind "The Lord is my protector. The Lord is with me. The Lord is my shepherd. The Lord will fight my battles. No weapon formed against me will prosper. Satan, you have no place here. Get out. Cameron, when you can talk, say those things with authority."

"Grandma, I was so scared. I knew I wasn't asleep, and this was not a dream, but it was happening to me. Will you pray that this never happens again? And please pray for me and Bella. Everybody knows Grandmothers can talk directly to God. Thank you; see you for the first Sunday dinner."

They hugged, and off he went.

CHURCH DUTIES

Grandma was a church trustee and it was an awesome job. They took care of anything from toilet paper to remodeling the building. Being a Trustee was a 24/7 labor of love.

She counted the offering on the second and fourth Sundays. For the last three weeks, someone had been putting lottery tickets in the church envelope and dropping them in the offering basket. They let the pastor know and asked if it was a winning ticket, was it a sin to cash it in for the winnings? To this date, there were no winning tickets. Someone had put a button in an envelope explaining it was solid gold and that was their offering. They wanted to include the value of the button in their yearly giving statement so they could report their generous contribution to the IRS. The gold-tone button was returned. Once there were keys to a Mercedes in the offering basket. The trustees were shocked thinking someone was donating their vehicle. After the service, the deacons informed them that a child had taken their mother's keys and dropped them in the basket. The mother didn't feel comfortable rummaging to the bottom of the basket looking for her keys. Once, the trustees flagged a counterfeit $20 bill. It simply didn't feel right when they were counting. There were a million interesting moments in that trustee room.

READY FOR THE DINNER

Sundays were special. Every first Sunday, Grandma prepared dinner for the family. She didn't care what they did the rest of the month, but she wanted to see all of them on the first Sunday. She let the triplets bring whoever they were dating so she could get a feel for their choices. They played board games and just enjoyed each other's company.

She did meal prep on Saturday night and partially cooked some of the food, so it would not take so long on Sunday. She bought and cut up a couple of chickens, seasoned them, and put them in the refrigerator. She chose to use her air fryer because it was healthier than greasy fried food. Jacob must have her signature nine cheese Macaroni and Cheese. She cooked it halfway; it would finish in the oven. Cornbread from scratch will brown on Sunday. She didn't have time to buy and pick greens, so they would have mixed vegetables. Garlic mashed potatoes and gravy for the lactose-intolerant folks who couldn't eat the Macaroni and Cheese. She could make sweet potato pies in her sleep. The stand-alone mixer made sure all the lumps were out and the pie melted in their mouths. She would surprise the kids with Ice cream. Roy would be looking for sweet iced tea. She was exhausted but ready for Sunday dinner. She sat down to relax.

The phone rang and there was a sweet kind voice; "Hello, I hope this is a better time to call. This is Ivy."

"Ivy, yes, I remember you from Madison's funeral."

"That's right. How are you doing today?"

She was glad to hear from her." Oh, baby, I'm doing well. How 'bout you?"

Ivy pretended to cry. "I've seen better days."

"Come on now, what's wrong?"

"My husband and I had a terrible fight. I just needed a deviation from him so I thought I would check on you."

Her protective mother instincts kicked in. She listened as Ivy talked about how her husband did not work. He sat around all day and played video games. He expected her to cook or pick up dinner every day. He did not value her or her time.

After about half an hour, she stopped talking about her husband. "Ma'am, if you are on Social Media, I would love to add you as my friend."

"Yes, I have an account to keep an eye on my grandkids. I don't use it too much." She gave her the account name. She continued, "Ivy, it was so sweet of you to check on me today. What are you doing tomorrow after church?"

Ivy seemed puzzled. "I don't usually go to church."

Bingo, this was Grandma's opportunity to witness. "Please be my guest at church tomorrow, and then you can come to my house for dinner and fellowship with my family. How would you like that?"

Ivy was excited. "Oh, that sounds nice. I look forward to seeing you tomorrow. Thank you for the invitation, goodbye."

Grandma had a splendid feeling about being a listening ear for Ivy. She wanted to know more about her connection to Madison.

44

FIRST SUNDAY

At church, the choir was on fire. Grandma always sat in the front so she can see and feel everything. Roy sat next to her. The director must have jumped five feet in the air while directing. The organ was grinding loud and the spirit was high. She cherished her church. Jacob and his family sat near the back. She kept looking for Ivy but didn't spot her. After church, Grandma was asked to stay to help count the offering.

"I can't. You know I don't count money on the first Sundays. I have plans. Today is Sandra's day. Where is she?"

The Chairman of the Trustee Board responded. "Didn't you hear? She was on a ladder trying to change the battery in her smoke detector, fell off the ladder, and broke her hip. Her granddaughter, Sha, put her in a nursing home. You know, once you go to one of those places; you lose your independence and are restricted. It's downhill from there. Girl, I don't trust Sha, she will take all of Sandra's money and leave her in there to rot."

"No, I didn't know about Sandra. I will check on her. Thanks for telling me. My family is waiting. We'll talk later." She saw Ivy walking toward her.

"I'm sorry I was late. The ushers directed me to where you were sitting, but I didn't want to disturb the service by coming to the front."

"It's OK Ivy. I'm glad you were able to make it. Now you know where I live since you were at my husband's repast at the house. I will see you there in a few minutes."

As Ivy walked away, Cameron whispered. "Grandma, who was that lady?"

"She is Madison's friend. I met her at the funeral. I invited her to dinner today."

He was surprised. "You did what? You don't even know her. I am getting bad vibes about her. You've got to stop thinking everyone is nice as you are. There are some bad people out there. I don't like it, can you uninvite her?"

"No, I will not uninvite her. It will be OK."

She was annoyed because her grandson was treating her like a child. She recognized and appreciated that he had the gift of discernment. He was an empath and when he is still and listened to God, he revealed things. When he was about seven, he told Grandma that he could move things by looking at them. He stared at the curtains for a while, making them move as if the wind was blowing. He tried to bend a fork like something he saw on television, but it didn't work, however, it was very hot. Once he told her that his little friend at school was going to fall out of a tree and break her arm. The very next day, it happened just like he described. She started paying attention to everything he said. About a week before Madison had her fatal car accident, Cameron told her to remind Madison to wear her seat belt and to drive carefully.

When Ivy got in her car she called her husband, Ken. "OK, I am in. I am going to her house now. She trusts me. We will make this family pay for the way Madison hurt us."

"You are the perfect person to do it because she will remember me. Mrs. Michelle is very gullible and is always trying to help and mother someone. It will be like taking candy from a baby. She will not see it coming. Go do it, babe."

"Because of Madison, we lost everything. My job at the hospital only keeps us afloat. I want revenge."

Grandma drove straight home. She knew her bunch well; they would want to eat as soon as they hit the door. When she came in, as usual, she closed the door but didn't lock it. She kicked off her shoes and put on her slides. She went to the kitchen, tied on the apron, and finished cooking the meal. Her brother, Roy, was the first one to arrive.

"Hey Sis, how about some sweet tea?"

"Now, don't worry my nerves, you know where everything is. Grab a glass and get it out of the refrigerator."

Next entered Jacob, Emily, and the precious grandbabies. More hugs from them all. Kayla brought her best friend, Nancy. Kimberly didn't bring anyone, and Cameron brought a girl she had not seen before.

She asked Cameron, "Who is this attractive young lady you brought with you?"

"This is Bella. We go to different schools and she is cool."

Bella smiled and extended her hand for a handshake. Grandma gave her a big hug and told her to come on in, then gave Cameron the *side-eye* hoping she was as sweet as he thinks. Grandma loves a house full. First Sundays are the best. The only one missing was Madison.

Kayla announced, "I brought a chess game. After dinner, I want to teach everyone how to play. I enjoy playing and I am thinking of playing in tournaments."

Kimberly retorted, "I don't think so. I have trouble with UNO. Chess is for smart people, and that's not us."

Everyone laughed.

"Kimberly, I can teach you." Then she turned her attention to her friend. "Nancy, will you play if no one else does?"

Nancy opened her mouth to respond but Roy spoke in a booming voice that overshadowed Nancy. "Kayla, I know how to play, and after dinner, I will kick your butt and make you say thank you."

Everyone *"ooohed"* at the trash-talking. Nancy looked offended and puffed up her chest, raised her head, and squinted her eyes to let Roy know she was about to respond. She quickly recoiled. Grandma took a note; that girl has a temper, recognizing that slight burst of assertion.

Roy sounded off. "Let's start eating that yard bird."

Grandma responded, "We have to wait; I invited one of Madison's friends. She was at church today."

"Is that the lady you were talking to after church?" Emily questioned.

"Yes, that was her."

"I've seen her before. She was at Dad's and Madison's repast. I believe she was with a man at Dad's repast."

"That's right, she was with her husband. Funny, I don't remember her or her husband."

Ivy knocked on the door. Several folks yelled in unison "Come in, it's open." She entered with a big smile. Grandma introduced Ivy to everyone.

Ivy needed to use the restroom badly. Grandma led her down the hall, pointed to the door, and went back to join the family.

Roy was persistent. "Enough of that talking, let's eat."

When Ivy joined them, she blessed the food.

Dear God, thank you for this food we are about to receive.

May this food serve as the nourishment of our bodies.

We pray for those who are less fortunate

and have food insecurities. Amen.

It was on. Everyone grabbed a plate and went around the kitchen getting what they wanted from the pots and pans on the stove and countertops. No one fixed anyone's plate and the only things on the table were the plates everyone was eating from. No fancy table setting or passing of the food; everyone got what they could eat, sat down, and ate.

Cameron inquired, "Grandma, where are the greens?"

"I didn't have time to pick greens, so eat these vegetables."

There was a lot of conversation at the table. Her son, Jacob, was excited about the 5-Sir Company driving job. Now they were giving him a local route that allowed him to come home every night. He said he had to go through a lot of security to drive the vaccine to different areas in Michigan. He beamed with pride because he was finally making enough money and be out of debt soon. Grandma was so proud of him. Lord knows she had prayed so many prayers to keep him out of the streets. The neighborhood influence could be so alluring. Most of his friends were either dead or in jail. The prayers of the righteous prevailed much. Meanwhile, Emily was growing more frustrated with Kimberly's attitude. Grandma had to separate them at the table.

"Kimberly, you sit near me, and Emily you can stay near your dad. You two have got to reach a truce."

"Ma it is bad. They got into a fistfight the other night." Jacob confessed.

"What? Emily, you better not tell me you hit this child with your fist. And Kimberly, I know you didn't rise up to your mother. You two should go to counseling. They have conflict resolution techniques that will help. Emily, I love you like a daughter, but don't you dare hit my grandchild again, or I will mess you up and pray over your body."

The family laughed. The kids snickered when she said "mess you up" which she heard in a movie. The guests raised their eyebrows.

Emily defended herself, "I had to protect myself. I was not going to let her punch me in the face and hit me with a baseball bat and not try to stop her."

Grandma was in shock. "What in the world is going on? Kimberly, call me tomorrow after school. Now, that's enough about you two, we have guests who don't understand our crazy."

Sheepishly, Kimberly replied, "OK Grandma, I will call you."

After dinner, Ivy helped with the dishes while the other family members debated politics and social injustices.

"Ivy, I didn't remember Madison talking about your friendship. How did you two meet?"

"We both worked at Ford Motor Company. I didn't know her that well, but we were always talking and laughing when we met in the cafeteria for lunch. We've had wonderful conversations. She worked in Information Technology and I worked in the Maintenance department. I quit and started working at Ascension Hospital. Madison adored you and I would like to get to know you better. I am not trying to take her place, but whenever you need company, please call me. My mother passed last year, and I miss her every day."

Grandma was touched. "Of course, I would like that. We can go to lunch sometime. Madison and I used to walk along the Downtown River. Would you like to do that someday? It feels strange walking without her."

"Yes, I would love to do that. How about tomorrow morning?"

"Hold on now. I have to rest on Monday, but Tuesday might be better. I'll call you to confirm a time. I'm so glad you are going to go walking with me."

"Enough talking and joking around, I am ready for a serious game of UNO. Put away that foolish Chess game and everybody come in the dining room for UNO." Kimberly yelled.

Roy and Kayla were in the back room where it was quiet and had just finished their chess game. Kayla was glad she almost beat him and vowed next first Sunday, she would win.

Kimberly continued like the game police, "Grandma, please stop washing the dishes, you and Ms. Ivy come and take a seat. Cameron, you and that girl can play too. Stop being so lovey-dovey and join your family. Somebody go get my daddy, he is probably on the porch smoking. Sis, what's up with your friend, Nancy, sitting in a corner by herself? She can pull up a chair and join us."

Cameron replied, "OK Kimberly, you made your point I will be glad to take you to school. Let's do this. Bella, would you like to play UNO?

"No, I don't play games."

Kimberly clapped back. "I bet you do play games. You are playing one right now. I don't see why Cameron likes you. You played with every guy in your school. I saw those pictures on social media. You don't play games? Please."

Everyone gasped. Kimberly did not have a filter. Cameron looked shocked but remained composed. It was clear that he didn't get those naked pictures.

Grandma stopped her precious grandchild. "Kimberly, that's enough. Rule your emotions, don't let them rule you." She winked at her hoping she would remember their past conversation. "My apologies, Bella, Ivy, and Nancy."

While the others started the first game, Grandma sat next to Bella on the sofa and gave her a glass of Sweet Tea. They talked about her school and the after-school activities. She enjoyed being a cheerleader. They chatted for a while then Ivy sat next to Bella and they began talking. They hit it off very well. Grandma was glad that shy Bella opened up to Ivy.

Ivy excused herself to go to the bathroom again. She was taking a long time. Grandma went to check on her. To get to the bathroom, she had to pass the office. The door was always kept tightly closed because of the confidential information regarding herself and Madison.

Her intuition told her to wait at the end of the hall to make sure Ivy was not going into the office. She got a tickle in her belly when

Ivy came down the hallway and rejoined Bella on the sofa. She looked at Cameron, he smiled and winked. She knew that he got the tickle in his belly again and that she was not trustworthy. That was how the spirit sometimes warned of danger. She believed her grandson, was right. There was something wrong about Ivy.

When the group was in high trash-talking gear, Ivy and Bella were in deep conversation. On the way to tidy the kitchen, Grandma noticed that the tightly closed office door was cracked open. She decided to delay the kitchen clean-up and listen to what Ivy was talking about.

Just then, Kimberly yelled, "Somebody please get my dad off the porch, he is the only true competitor in this family."

Grandma got within earshot of Ivy and Bella with her back turned but with ears wide open she heard Ivy say "yes, everything is fine. I might have to return a few more times."

What was she talking about? Could it be a doctor's appointment? She kept her eyes on Ivy for the remainder of the day.

Grandma went on the porch to get Jacob. He was smoking a cigarette and on the phone talking low. She heard part of his conversation about driving the vaccine to a certain location.

"Why are you talking about work? It's Sunday and you are not working today. Did you get a new phone? I haven't seen that one."

"This is my work phone. I am getting ready for work tomorrow." He hung up and joined the family.

What Grandma didn't know was that Jacob had been on the phone with Drake. They were planning an elaborate heist of the vaccine. Drake educated Jacob about some of the moving parts. He promised Jacob a million dollars. They would talk later about the details.

After playing UNO, the family got dangerous with Spades. Jacob came to life, and Roy was all in. They made perfect partners. Cameron was trying to hang with the trash-talking. Surprisingly, little aloof Nancy was slamming the cards like a man. She played very well. She acted like she didn't need Cameron as her partner. She knew when to cut and when to throw off. She tried to break the glass table the way she slammed the cards down and talked smack. It was a competition to determine who could slam the cards the hardest. Nancy was proving herself a worthy contender. Kimberly fancied the bantering and was egging on Cameron.

Grandma sat back and relished the moment. Most of the ladies migrated to the sunroom where they drank tea and talked about social issues like the recent shootings and medical discoveries. Ivy and Bella stayed huddled together and started a game of dominoes. She saw Bella give Ivy a piece of paper. They probably exchanged phone numbers. Kayla, Emily, and Grandma enjoyed a few laughs. In group settings, Kayla usually listens more than she talks. She wondered what she and her friend, Nancy, talked about. Nancy probably carried the conversations. Emily liked not being a mom for a few minutes and found comfort in being away from Kimberly's smart mouth.

Grandma was getting tired. After she finished cleaning the kitchen everyone heard those dreaded words, "After this last game, it's time to go."

As usual, there were a few grunts and groans then the whole crew left together after lots of hugs and kisses.

She went back to the office, and the door was opened even more. She couldn't tell if anything was missing but nothing was out of place. She needed to find out more about this Ivy girl. She would not be invited back to this house.

She got on her knees and prayed her bedtime prayer.

Dear Lord, thank you for my family. I love them dearly.

God, this girl, Ivy, is a concern.

I welcomed her into my heart and my home,

but I don't have a good feeling about her.

God, you gave me discernment

and I can usually feel when someone is not right.

I believe I let my grief and feelings about Madison's death

cloud my rational judgment.

I ask that you show me if she is up to no good.

Dear God, about my brother Roy. I know he is

having trouble with his health.

Please give him some relief.

Show him what he needs to do to ease the pain.

Dear God, I thank you for Jacob and his new position.

I pray that he has your favor while working.

Thank you for keeping your arms around my grandbabies.

Amen.

KEN/IVY

When Ivy got home from the First Sunday dinner, she was excited to share it with her husband, Ken. "Babe, I got some of the records. She is an excellent record keeper, and her file cabinet was not locked. I was able to go through her files quickly. There were lots of papers sitting on top of the desk. I took pictures with my phone. I got her bank account number, social security number, and Medicare information. We already had her legal name, address, and phone number. I copied her license plate number. Since you know the financial industry, you can take it from here."

"Great. Remember, you have to keep in contact with her, go on walks, call her and play like a good girl. Even tag her in a post on social media. Now it is time for me to get to work. I will take care of her Social Security checks, and bank accounts. I will also make a few accounts with her driver's license and social security number before I sell her information on the Dark Web Marketplace. That Marketplace will give me $5.00 for her name and social security number, $35.00 for one credit card number, and expiration date, $65.00 for her Facebook information, and $100 for her driver's license information. The Dark Web Marketplace will sell everything to thousands of people. They will make a fortune off her and she won't see it coming."

With greed in his eyes, he lovingly asks Ivy, "Is there anything you want me to buy for you using her credit cards?"

"I could use a new car."

"Don't get greedy, they can trace that back. We'll get clothes and electronics."

JACOB/DRAKE

Jacob called Drake to continue the conversation from his mother's house. "Hey man, I'm sorry I had to cut the phone call short earlier today. We go a long way back and you know how the first Sunday dinners are. You didn't finish telling me about the guys in the transfer truck."

Drake didn't like that Jacob terminated the conversation before he was finished. He was the mastermind in this job, and he deserved respect. Drake had street cred and did time in Federal and State prisons. He was the one who ends the conversation, not Jacob.

In a calm voice, Drake responded, "No problem about the abrupt ending. I got guys from a previous job I did in Detroit a few months ago. They are professional. You will interact with them briefly. Now, let's go over the details on your end."

Jacob began, "On Saturdays, the load is the biggest and there is no security on the truck. I will drive to the location. There is no need for the refrigerated truck because the new vaccine is combined with the booster, and it can be kept at room temperature. Drake, are you sure we can do this?"

"My associates got the refrigerated truck just to be on the safe side."

"What about the plane and the ability to transport it to South Sudan in the Motherland?"

Drake took a long draw from his inhaler. "Jacob, you are stressing. I've done business with the people in South Sudan who make things happen. They regularly purchase my products. I know them and they trust me. This is a win-win situation. They get the vaccine and we get the money. They came to me to help their people. We have a great working relationship, there is honor among thieves. They will do what I tell them. Now, I flew here from California to make sure you have your ducks in a row."

Drake paused then continued. "I am so sorry I didn't get a chance to go to the funeral, but I did sneak a peek at the funeral home the day before. Madison looked beautiful."

Jacob was noticeably aggravated. "Hey, keep my sister's name out of your mouth. We won't discuss this again. I'm not playing with you about my family." He took a deep breath to center himself and continued. "Drake, I am having second thoughts about doing this thing with you. I like my job and I make honest money to support my family."

"What man? Don't forget I pulled the strings to get you that job and that shift. If you think you are hurting the 5-Sir Company, think again. They made so much money from this vaccine and booster combination. They are not hurting at all. They tell the CDC when it is time for a vaccine or booster. The 5-Sir Company is the puppeteer, and the whole world is dancing."

Drake appealed to Jacob's soft side, "Anyway, don't you want to help the deprived people in South Sudan, Africa? They are not considered in the human being equation as important enough to attempt to get them the vaccine. They are dying like flies. I saw on the Internet that a reporter was sitting around a table full of people.

The head guy called the Black people in Africa expendable. Everyone at the table agreed. I was outraged. It's a calculated conspiracy to allow the people in Africa to die. That weighed heavy on my heart, and it should on yours too. There is no news coverage detailing their deaths. Africa has been ignored by the rest of the world. Just consider this your contribution to helping the Motherland."

Drake attempted to lighten the mood, "If we do this the way I planned, we will be rich, and you can move wherever you want and take care of everyone in your family in style. I know you are close to your family. How is your mother?"

Jacob lost his cool. "I'm not going to tell you again, leave my family out of the conversation."

Drake said, "Ok, ok, since I was once part of the family, I just wanted to know…"

Jacob interrupted, "Screw you Drake and kiss off. I'm done. We will talk tomorrow."

"Come on my brother, don't be a little girl. Let's talk like men. We have a job to do, and after that, you don't ever have to see me again.

"Bet."

Drake continued, "My Michigan associates mapped and studied this route for nine months. It's like we are birthing our child." He chuckled and continued. "This is going to happen next month on the 3rd, which is a Saturday. That gives us almost a month to perfect the plan and iron out the bumps. We will practice every Sunday on your day off."

"Every Sunday! That seems a bit extreme. I take the same route six times a week. It's a no-brainer."

"Stop whining and man up. We are doing this my way, timing is everything. Here is the plan. At 2:15 pm you will pick up your load in Rochester, Michigan for your scheduled route. Since they have trackers on the truck you will follow the route to the letter. When you reach the intersection of Rochester Road and Adams Road, there is an area where we will electronically disable the cameras on the city lights and the surrounding locations. Before Saturday, we will destroy the cameras of the nearby businesses and those tell-all doorbells. On Saturday, when you stop at the red light, the truck cab will pass under the viaduct, aka the bridge. Only half of the trailer will be under the viaduct away from cameras. The transfer truck will be completely under the viaduct. The transfer associates will be inside the trailer of the transfer truck. When you pull up to the light, they will shoot a tire. They will use an explosive to open the back door; then they will unload the vaccine and put it in their truck."

Drake took a puff from his Inhaler and went on with labored breathing: "You call the 5-Sir Company and tell them you must have run into a huge pothole, and you think you have damaged the tires and rims, and you are getting out to double-check. That will let them know why the tracker is still. We have about four minutes to clear the truck and drive away. That intersection has a three-minute light so that will buy us a little more time."

Drake took another puff from his inhaler and started coughing. "Since this has to look like a bona fide robbery; when you get out to look at the tires, they will cover your head. You will take a few punches then one of them will shoot you in your arm."

Jacob was stunned. "What? I didn't know I was going to be shot. I have kids and a wife who depends on me."

"Trust me, man, they are professionals, it will only be a flesh wound and they won't break any bones. We have to make this look good. After 10 or 15 minutes, the 5-Sir Company will send the police and someone to check on you. I planned this location because it is only five minutes away from the hospital and you will be in and out on the same day."

"Where will you be while I am getting beat up and shot?"

"I will wait for the transfer truck at the city airport with their private plane. I know the police are on my tail for trafficking in Los Angeles. I have to lay low. I can't be at the transfer site. Plan B: if there is a time restriction we will roll the entire truck on the plane. Trust me, man, nothing will go wrong."

Drake had a villainous smile on his face. It was almost audible. "When we deliver the truck to the plane, they will wire $10 million to my account. Once it is received, I will give the all-clear, and the flight will depart. I have already paid half to truck transfer associates, the folks to sequence the lights and cameras, and the local thugs who will smash the business cameras. Our South Sudan associates will pay for the plane and its people. I will wire the other half to everyone when I receive the $10 million. Once the product is loaded on the plane, our job is done. It is party time."

"Hey man, what about me? I didn't get half of anything. I'm the one taking the risks, getting beat up and shot. I want at least $10,000 now in my U.S. account before I do anything."

"That is not an issue, sorry I missed you. Text me your U.S. account number and it will be there the day before the job."

"I don't think so, send it now. This way I know there will not be Internet transmission problems. After the job, that night I want the agreed-upon $1 million wired into my overseas account I gave you last month. I'm not talking about that bitcoin, cryptocurrency stuff. I want US dollars."

"Everyone else is satisfied with crypto. Why do you have to be so special?"

"Because I don't trust it. Make it happen, Drake."

"Don't get your panties in a bunch. You will get yours in US dollars.

IVY/BELLA

Ivy called Bella to talk about the Sunday dinner. "The plan is coming together. I hope you didn't blow it at the Sunday dinner by being too lovey-dovey with Cameron and stan-offish with the rest of the family."

"Sis, don't worry, I've got him wrapped around my finger. I unlocked his phone and have all of his personal information and passwords. He trusts me and thinks I am timid and helpless. The poor thing wants to teach me everything."

They laughed.

"This is great! I can't believe the planned meeting at the mall worked. I had to follow him for a week to make sure I knew his schedule. And you, girl, bumping into him at the food court and wasting your soda was pure genius. That shy girl act worked. He wants to be your savior. We may be in-laws, but I consider you my little sister. When we are done with this family, they won't know what hit them. I talked to Ken, and he is going to take care of stealing their identities and cleaning them out financially. Your brother is geeked about this whole thing and is glad you are working with us because we can't trust everyone."

"Ken and I were never that close as siblings growing up. I feel closer to you than to him. But every time I think about what dead

Madison did to him, I want to shoot up that house on the First Sunday when everyone is inside."

"Now, hold on little grasshopper. We are smarter than that. Remember, we have a plan, and we will stick to it. Give Ken all your information on Cameron by the 15th. My information combined with yours will be enough to blast them to kingdom come. Everything will hit the fan on the 30th when her social security check is missing. We will be invited to the First Sunday dinner to witness their reaction."

KAYLA/NANCY

"Kayla when are going to tell your family?" Nancy inquired. "Girl, it's not that easy. You've met my family; they are a special group. I am not sure how they would react if I told them I was gay, and you are my girlfriend."

"I've been like this all my life and when I finally told my mother she said, she knew I was gay when I was 3 years old and was waiting on me to discover it and then tell her. She said she didn't want to rush me and make me feel uncomfortable. So, Kay, it is my guess your family already has suspensions. We've been together for a year and when prom comes, I want to take you. It's time we are out in the open."

"I know you are right, but I am afraid."

"Kay, do you love me?"

"Yes Nancy, you know I do."

"Then why is this so hard for you to do? We are young, and we will be together forever. The sooner everyone knows and respects our union, the better. We will be free to hold hands at the mall and in school. And I can kiss you in front of everyone."

"I am not ready; don't force me to come out. I don't know what to say to my parents. My dad will freak out. I've heard him say stuff like, God made Adam and Eve, not Adam and Steve. His favorite is God didn't make a mistake and these confused people have been molested as children. He calls the gay community terrible names. I go into my room and scream into my pillow every time he talks like that. I want to go on the defensive, but I am afraid. I need to come up with a plan to tell them. I saw some ideas on the Internet about *How to come out to your Parents*. Maybe I can write them a letter and put it under their bedroom door and wait for them to talk to me? Or better yet, to be more personal I can do a video and email it to each of them. I went on an LGBTQ+ website and they gave excellent advice. It's nice to know I am not the only teen struggling."

"I have an idea. Your grandmother seems cool. I can't believe she was going to beat down your mother because she hit your smart-mouth sister. Now that's some talk show, prime-time TV stuff. Your grandmother loves you guys. Why don't you start with her and see how it goes? I am sure she will be accepting. Of course, you can expect some negativity, but it will not last because you have such a close and loving family."

"I will give it some thought. Knowing my grandma, she will quote scriptures and tell me I am sinning. But I don't like living a lie and I want to be free to love you."

"We can get some scriptures too. Somewhere in Genesis, the first chapter of the bible says, '*So God created man in his own image, he created him, created male and female he created them.*' So why would God make a man person first, then create a male and female person? This tells me that both a male and a female are in a person. So, you can be in a female body and have male hormones. Or you can be in a male body and have female hormones. Get your grandmother to explain that!"

"That is interesting. I will certainly give it some thought. Thanks."

CAMERON/BELLA

Every time he thought about Bella, his stomach quivered. He remembered his grandmother saying *that's the Holy Spirit trying to get your attention.* Or was this love? Were the quivers the butterflies everyone talks about? He was falling in love with her. She needed him and he liked being the one she depended on. But there was something about her that didn't seem right. He collected his thoughts and asked God to give him discernment about Bella. After a few minutes, he opened his phone to check his social media. The phone was doing an update, so he waited longer than usual. The update must have whipped out his password because his phone was wide open for anyone to look at his information. He quickly reinstated his password. While thumbing through social media a thought kept urging him to go to Bella's page. Oh, there she was, so beautiful with that shy smile. She only had 25 followers. That was not surprising because she was so shy. All of them were probably her family.

He remembered an episode of "Tech Talk" where they used one of the photos on social media and researched to see if there was another page connected. Something urged him to search. He used one of the few pictures in her photo library.

Bam, the search produced another page called Bella the Baller. *What the hell*? She had over four thousand followers. They were mostly men. There was one woman who commented daily. It was Ivy. This was the lady his grandmother invited to church and the house. He thought they met for the first time at his grandmother's house. He spent hours on Bella's "Baller" page reading the comments between Ms. Bella the Baller and Ivy. There were pictures of his shy girl dressed like a slut. Her boobs and butt were hanging out. She was twerking and shaking her big, beautiful, bubble-luscious butt. There were hundreds of graphic comments from men describing what they wanted to do to her. She even had a video pleasuring herself. Oh no, this was not the same girl he respected. He could not believe it. She was smoking the biggest blunt right in the picture. *Yes, she is a baller alright.* How could he not know this? In a picture, she was holding lots of money and said that "her day was coming" and that "she would be paid ten times the amount shown". This was too much to take. It broke his heart. Then he remembered what his grandmother told him about being a gentleman when he wanted to get rid of her.

He distanced himself. When she sent her daily morning text just to say hi, he sent a simple text that he was busy and that they would talk later. On the third day after seeing "Bella the Baller" on social media, he was clear-minded and decided to give her a call. He knew he had to be smart and not let her know he was aware of her double identity. He didn't trust her and needed to get her out of his life in a way that she wouldn't be angry and stalk him.

"Hello Bella, how are you doing?"

"I am hanging in there. I've missed talking to you. School is tough and sometimes I feel like I can't make it. Some of the kids are teasing me, mostly boys. I am afraid to walk home from school alone.

Babe, do you think you can come to my school and walk with me tomorrow?"

"Sweetheart, I need to talk to you about something very important. You know how I feel about you. You are the best thing that ever happened to me. I think about you all of the time. Babe, we need to take a step back because my grades are falling because I am not concentrating on my studies. The SAT is coming up and I need to focus. I bought a prep test book that has eight sample tests and I need to concentrate so I can get into one of the top ten colleges. After the tests, let's regroup and see how we are jelling. What do you think?"

"Cameron, I understand because I am studying for the same test, but that is no reason to break up with me. We can study together. It will be great. We can help each other. Come on babe, don't you think this is a good idea? I need you to keep me on track. You are the only one I have in my corner."

"Bella, I can't study with you around. Give me some space. I am sure afterward we will find our new normal."

Bella was noticeably upset. "Well Cameron, it looks like you had your mind made up before you called. Do you have another girl? Whatever! It is what it is. You are not the only one who wants my time. Whenever you decide you want me back, I might not be available. So, it would be in your best interest to keep me while you have me."

"I've never heard you talk like that. I thought you were shy and only dated me. Thank you, Miss. Baller, for showing me who you are."

"What did you just call me?"

"I called you Miss Bella. What do you think I said?"

"Oh nothing, that is what I heard. OK, Cameron, have a nice life, goodbye."

She hung up before Cameron could say bye. Cameron chuckled because he knew he called her Miss Baller just to get her reaction. She was out of his life, now he had to tell his grandmother that the dynamic duel at First Sunday dinner was not their first meeting.

KAYLA/GRANDMA

Kayla was going to come out to her grandmother. "Hello Grandma, how are you doing?"

"It is so nice to get a phone call from you. I am doing fine baby. What's going on with you?"

"If you're not busy tomorrow, can I come by after school and chop it up with you?"

"Chop it up? Is that the new way of saying you want to talk?" She laughed. "Sure, after you get the OK from your parents, stop by and we will chop it up. Do you want me to cook dinner for you?"

"No Grandma, I will eat when I get home. Do you want me to pick up something for you?"

"Now that is sweet. You don't work, you don't have any money, and how can you pick up something for me? Thank you, baby, see you tomorrow." *That girl never opens up. I wonder what's going on. I know she got her period a couple of months ago. Her mother, Emily, said she was doing fine with her emotions. Maybe she needs some boyfriend advice. Maybe she's pregnant. Lord no, that can't be it. It's probably the school SAT jitters. I'll bet Kimberly's smart mouth is getting on her nerves. I will drive myself crazy wondering what she wants to talk about. I will make her favorite, spaghetti with melted cheese on top. She loves Texas toast. That will get that little girl talking.*

Like clockwork, immediately after school, the doorbell rang, it was Kayla. "Hey, Grandma."

"Hi baby, hug my neck. Pull off your wraps and have a seat."

"Do I smell spaghetti?"

"Yes, you do, and Texas toast."

"You didn't have to cook for me. I told you I would eat when I got home, but since you made it, yes please, I am starving."

They both laughed.

"I had to cook for myself anyway, so I made some extra for you. Go ahead and have as much as you want."

After digging in, they started to talk.

"Ok Kayla, I know something is bothering you. Whatever it is, you know I always have your best interest. So, don't be afraid, tell me. What's on your mind child? Spit it out."

"This is so hard to say. Grandma, times have changed since you were young. I've been thinking about how to say this, but I can't find the words. I've gone over this a million times in my head while on the bus coming here. I am not ready. I can't say it." She put down her fork and took a few deep breaths. She closed her eyes and tried not to let the tears fall. Her silent torment was amplified by the tears bursting through her tightly closed eyes. She was afraid of rejection.

"We can work it out, you go ahead until you are all cried out, then we can talk,"

Grandma continued to eat. Then Kayla started eating again. Grandma raised her eyebrows and wondered what in the world was going on. She wanted to grab her by the collar, shake her, and make her talk. But that is not what a grandmother does.

Kayla took a deep breath, and with her head lowered looking at her spaghetti, she lifted her eyes and said, "Grandma, I believe I am gay."

Grandma dropped her fork on the floor; it bounced a few times and stopped standing straight up in the corner. Then she felt a *rushing mighty wind* that took her breath away and almost knocked her out of the chair. The room started spinning. She had a hot flash, which felt like hell itself; sweat was dripping from her brow and neck and then sliding down her back and chest. She was in shock and couldn't breathe.

She thought she would pass out because of the avalanche of emotions. Then she looked at the child's distorted face from the pain of the admittance. She had the biggest tear tracks down her face. There was snot was running down from both nostrils between her lip. Like a magician, Grandma whipped out a hankie she kept under her left sleeve. In a calm voice, she said "use this to wipe your eyes and nose." Then she said, in a matter-of-fact way, "Why do you believe that?"

"Because I like girls and the thought of a boy touching or kissing me makes me want to throw up."

"There are a lot of girls I like. I have friends from high school. We've been friends for fifty-five years. I love those crazy girls, but I am not in love with them. Maybe this is how you feel about girls?"

"No Grandma, I am in love with Nancy."

"Are you sure, or do you love her like your friend, and Nancy's suggestions are confusing to you? She has a strong and persuasive personality."

"No grandma. She is my friend, but she is also my lover."

"You are only seventeen, what do you know about a lover and intimacy? Wait, don't answer that. I don't want to know the details about that part of your life. But I do want more details about why you think you are gay. Is it this one girl, Nancy, or have you thought about kissing girls all of your life? How long have you felt like this?"

"Slow down, let me answer. I've always thought about kissing girls ever since I can remember. And yes, Nancy is my first girlfriend. She told her family she was gay a long time ago."

"Kayla, I would not be a Christian if I didn't tell you what the word of God says about this. God intended for men and women to be together. This type of intimacy between you and Nancy is not natural or normal and not what God wants."

"It feels natural to me and Nancy. I knew you would say something like that, so I have Scriptures to prove my point. Genesis Chapter one, verse twenty-seven the B part of the scripture says, *male and female created them.* So, Grandma, God created me a female, but he knew I would have male hormones and have feelings for another female."

"Hmmm, Kayla, I am impressed that you searched the bible for that passage. I am very familiar with that scripture. Yes, verse seventeen does say that, but did you read verse twenty-eight?"

"No, I didn't."

"Well, let's read it."

Grandma got her Bible, opened it and pointed to the verse, and asked her to read it. Kayla began reading slowly.

"And God blessed them, and God said to them be fruitful and multiply, replenish the earth and subdue it."

Grandma interrupted, "That's enough. In another scripture, God calls it an abomination, and unnatural. Now you tell me how can two women be fruitful and multiply to replenish the earth without anything coming from a man? Either the man pumps in that seed or it is planted in the woman. But the seed must come from a man. I know that scientists are telling women they need a complete hysterectomy and are harvesting the uterus and experimenting with planting them in men or Transgender women, so they can carry a baby. But at this present date, we know a man does not have the equipment to carry a baby. Honey, if you look at it, everything grows from a seed. If you want a peach tree, you plant a peach seed. Now, I don't eat seedless grapes or seedless watermelon because that's not natural. The seed contains life. How can two of the same sex replenish the earth without the seed of a man and the soil of a woman's womb for the seed to grow into a baby? Civilization would die."

"I don't know Grandma. All I know is that I am in love with Nancy."

"I get it, sweetie. I wanted to show you that scripture. My take on the whole gay world is that God made you and I love every living thing God made, except roaches. It is not up to me to try to force you to see things the way I see them. If God does not like your choices, that is between you and God, not me or anyone else. Kayla, I love you no matter what 'title' anyone places on you. Now about your parents, it will be a tall order to educate them and come out. Now that I think about it, why is it important to tell anyone? That is your business. I don't understand why there has to be an announcement that a person is gay. People who are not gay don't go around telling everyone, I'm not gay and I sleep with whomever. If someone says they are gay, the response should be, fine. Kayla, just live your life."

"Grandma, I don't have answers. I just know how I feel. It's a liberating feeling to be accepted. I am going to participate in the Gay Pride parade. I want to be around more people who are like me."

"Ok, baby, I am rambling on. I understand and accept that you are gay, and you will be that way. I want to be socially correct. What do I call you? A lesbian, homosexual or gay? What do the letters LGBTQ mean?"

"That's funny! Just call me your granddaughter. The acronym LGBTQ+ stands for Lesbian, Gay, Bisexual, Transgender, Queer, and more, including Intersex and Ally."

"Baby, when I was growing up, if we called someone Queer, it was considered offensive and insensitive which usually resulted in a fight. Are you telling me, now that calling someone Queer is acceptable? Nope, I am not saying that word. Another thing, something about the acronym does not seem right with all of those letters. If two females are together, they are called lesbians and can be referred to using any of those letters. If the letter L for lesbians exclusively references women, what is the letter that exclusively references men? I know there are lots of organizations to support gay teens. I saw it on the morning talk show. I don't have a clue how to help you with this. But rest assured, if you need me, I will be on your side. I respect you for standing up for what you want. One more question, who determines which one takes the more masculine role? I have a feeling Nancy has more masculine energy than you. As long as Nancy or anyone else is nice to you I don't have a concern. But if she thinks she has to slap you around to prove she is equal to a man, then we have a big problem. When do you plan to tell your parents?"

"I wanted you to help me figure that out."

"Since they are around you more than I am, they might already know it and waiting on you to say something."

"Nope, not dad, he is a gay basher. He calls gay people terrible names. He says they are not Christians and going to hell. He goes off the deep end whenever anyone talks about gay rights."

"Let's think this out. You kids are seventeen and will be graduating soon and going off to college. Do you want to tell them before you go or just let it ride through the summer and live your life in college?"

"I didn't think about that. They don't have to know because I will be gone in a year. I've held it in for all of my life, certainly, one year won't kill me. But one issue, Nancy wants to take me to the prom when we graduate in June. So, I've got to tell them."

"I've heard that groups of girls go to the prom together. That could be an option."

Kayla smiled and nodded. Then she helped to tidy the kitchen and hugged her. During the hug, Grandma said a quick prayer.

Dear God, I ask that you protect my grandchild.

She has so many emotions going on.

Lord, give her clarity to express herself.

Please let the world be kind and more understanding.

God, I don't understand everything she is feeling right now,

but I pray that she finds peace knowing that you understand her.

I pray for a more accepting world and that she

is judged by her character

and not by a title someone gives her.
God, please strengthen her.
I pray that one day when someone says they
are gay that the response is acceptance.
I pray that it will not be a big deal.
I pray that Christians will allow God to judge each human
and realize it is not up to us to do so.
We are not qualified to be fruit inspectors
inspecting the fruits of anyone's life,
that is up to you, God. Amen.

After the prayer, Kayla was happily on her way home.

JACOB/ DRAKE

Jacob was busy doing the honey-do list Emily made the night before. While doing the yard work he needed to call Drake at the agreed-upon time. Before he started dialing, his son Cameron joined him to help do the work to have a man-to-man talk. He wanted to know when he knew his mother was the one for him. Jacob was glad his son came to him and the gangsters in the street. As they talked, they worked. They changed light bulbs in the hall, tightened screws on the kitchen cabinets, stopped the leaking faucet, oiled the squeaking doors, and changed the batteries in the smoke detectors. The conversation flowed easily. Jacob explained how they met, and he knew he wanted to marry her the day they met.

Cameron told his dad about Bella. He explained that he thought he was falling in love with her because he got the butterflies when he saw her, even though they were taking a break. Jacob listened to his son very closely. He told Cameron to be careful and to guard his heart until he was sure about this girl. Cameron was satisfied with their man-to-man talk and went to his room to play video games. He was confident he made the right decision about Bella.

Jacob went into the garage to hide and call Drake. He was nervous about being late making the call.

As he pulled out his burner phone, Emily came into the garage. "Jacob, I appreciate you for taking care of the things on my list. There is nothing sexier than a man working around the house. It turned me on. We can lock the garage door and I will give you that extra special thing you like."

Jacob was surprised at her reaction. But his body responded, and they felt like kids tiptoeing around when they were in the garage having a quickie. Sneaking made it more intense, and they came at the same time trying not to scream while in their ecstasy. After their intimacy, he decided he would find more things to fix around the house.

Emily left the garage with a smile as big as outdoors.

Jacob looked at the time. He was very late making the phone call. "Hey man, I apologize for the time, but something came up."

Jacob chuckled inside because he latterly came up for Emily. "So, let's meet on Sunday about a block away from the 5-Sir Company. Do you have my money? It's getting close to the job time." Jacob heard heavy breathing not knowing that Drake was hooked up to his breathing machine.

Drake responded. "Let me quarterback this thing. We will meet on the corner of Rochester Road and 5th."He stopped to take a puff from the inhaler. "I will tell my associates from the city to sync the lights so we can go through everyone except the one on Rochester Road and Adams. The light will be timed for 3 minutes, they will add an extra minute. Don't forget, we are going to do this every Sunday at 2:15 pm until they can do it in their sleep and we are comfortable doing everything in 4 minutes."

"Every time we talk, you say the same thing, I got it, I got it. I am not stupid."

"Bring your piece for extra protection."

"Protection against whom? Nothing is supposed to go wrong, right?"

"Right, it is best to have some heat as a backup."

"I'm biting off more than I can chew. I don't want to shoot anyone."

"If you do what I tell you, then you won't have to."

KEN/IVY

One thing Ivy didn't get was the password to Mrs. Michelle's bank account at Chase. Ken constructed a fake email with the bank's logo and sent it to her email address. He put her account number in the email and informed her that her account had been compromised and that she needed to reset her password.

Since Ken can write computer-coded programs, he created a fake bank website. When she clicks on the link in the email, it will take her to the fake website. When she changes her password, Ken will have access to her account. To seal the deal, Ken will send her a letter in the US mail to confirm the password change. The letter will give her a level of confidence that everything is legitimate. Once the password is received, he will open a business loan for $100,000. When the loan is secure, he will withdraw all of the funds. He and Ivy will run up the credit cards and open another credit card account at Virgin Money in the UK.

When the dust settles from moving the money, he will go to the post office and put in a permanent address change. The mail will be forwarded to an unknown location. Since he had her social media account and email address, he would hack her account and divert all her followers and contacts to a stripper site where he will place her face on a naked body and the backdrop will be her church. Ken called himself the Kingpin of the Internet.

Ken explained to Ivy how he would destroy the grandson, Cameron.

"Since we have the cell phone number, carrier, account number, and password, we can work directly with the carrier. I can hack his social media accounts and divert them to a fake American's most wanted page and Photoshop his picture all over the page. We can send out disgusting posts."

"What about the granddaughters?" She inquired.

"We don't have anything on them, so we will let them slide. Babe, I'm ravenous. Did you pick up anything for dinner?"

Ivy sucked her teeth, rolled her eyes, and then stormed out the door in search of dinner.

IVY/BELLA

While driving to pick up dinner Ivy got a phone call from Bella. She wanted to chat over a drink. Ivy welcomed this deviation. It prolonged the time she had to go back to Ken.

The restaurant/club Floods was their meeting spot. It was where the up-and-coming professionals gathered. They arrived at the same time; the embrace was warm then they walked into the club. The best table was near the window in the back. Ivy ordered a vodka spritz and Bella ordered Cognac.

Bella started talking as soon as they sat down. "I broke up with Cameron."

"Oh no, what happened?"

"He said he wanted to take a break to study. I got a feeling it was something more and he was being polite."

"That's OK. We have his information. You did your job and we have enough. I will let your brother know that you are out of the picture and your job is complete. I guess I won't see you at the next First Sunday Dinner?"

They laughed.

"I guess not. Have fun and eat enough for me too."

Ivy noticed an older guy checking out Bella. He started walking toward their table. He said, he knew Bella and had seen her on the Internet. He sat down and motioned to the waitress that he wanted to order them another round. Ivy's instincts picked up that he was up to no good. She told him no thanks, and they left the club. Bella wanted to stay. She was only seventeen and should not have been drinking anyway. Ivy made sure Bella got in her car and drove away before she pulled off. Bella circled the block and went back into the club to find the guy.

CAMERON/GRANDMA

Cameron called his grandmother to tell her about Bella.

"Hey Grandma, what are you doing?"

"Watching TV, how are you doing, baby?"

"I have some interesting news for you."

"Wait, let me mute the TV, those darn furniture commercials are so loud."

"No, I think the car commercials are louder. When they come on, I instantly hit the mute button and just read what comes on the screen. I know they do it for effect, but I find it insulting to my ears when I am watching an exciting movie, and all of a sudden, here comes the commercial blasting the eardrums or waking me from a nap."

They both laughed.

"I thought it was just me. Thank God for the person who invented the mute button. Well, baby, let's chop it up."

Cameron laughed, "What do you know about chopping it up? You are too much. Remember the girl I brought to the Sunday Dinner, Bella?"

"Yes, she was kind of discreet and to herself."

"My gut was right. She is not who she represented herself to be. When Kimberly blurted out about her trashy pictures, she was right. I did some investigating on social media; I found out that she has a different site that she didn't tell me about. That site has all kinds of sexually explicit pictures and videos."

"Oh, my goodness!"

"That's not all; Bella and that girl Ivy knew each other before Sunday?"

"What, how could that be? Does your friend Bella have a connection with Ascension Hospital?"

"I don't know. We have only been seeing each other for a few months and the hospital never came up."

Grandma's intuition kicked in. "There is something fishy going on. That Ivy girl is not right. My gut tells me she went into my office on one of her trips to the bathroom."

"Come on Grandma, why would she do that, and why do you suspect her?"

Grandma knows every inch of her house. She keeps a tidy house, and everything has a place, and everything is in its place.

"Because I keep that door closed. When Ivy left the bathroom, I went to tidy up the kitchen and I noticed it was cracked open. I don't know if she went in there when she first came in rushing like she had to use the bathroom, or later when everyone was playing games, and no one was watching. But mark my word, she was in there."

She had Cameron's attention and he asked. "What do you think she was looking for?"

"I don't know. If she wanted stuff for Madison's memory, all she had to do was ask. I don't trust her, and she is not welcome in this house. If she calls again, I am going to tell her I know she was in there and to leave us alone."

"Wait Grandma, let's think this through. Until we figure out the connection between that Ivy girl and Bella, let's pretend nothing has happened. I've already told Bella I don't want to see her again so that door is closed. We need to keep the door open to Ivy. I'll do some digging around on social media. One of the guys in the youth department from the church goes to her school. I'll talk to him and meet him at their school to get more information about Bella. I knew something was not right with her because the first day I met her, my stomach quivered.

"Sho-Nuff! You do listen to what I say. I remember telling you about that stomach quivering a long time ago. Sometimes we listen and sometimes we get our head bumped for disobeying. Remember, when we read the bible and pray God puts it deep down in us so when the time comes, we can pull it out and learn from the experience. The preacher said partial obedience is total disobedience."

"Ok Grandma, I love you but, I don't want to hear a sermon right now. I will let you know what happens with my research. I feel like a private investigator. One more thing, let's not tell the rest of the family until the First Sunday dinner. By that time, we both should have some answers."

"Ivy and I are supposed to go to the river walk trail tomorrow. What should I tell her when she calls?"

"Tell her you've got a bad back and need to rest. That you've thrown it out before and will have to take it easy for about a month. That will keep her away from the house and she won't ask you to do anything."

"That is true. I do have a bad back. Well, look at you, a future private detective. That sounds like a plan. Alright, goodbye. We'll talk later. I love you."

"Bye grandma, I love you more."

JACOB/EMILY/JAMES

"Hey Jacob, babe, you've been working a lot lately. Maybe we can set aside some money to buy stuff for the kid's dorm room when they go off to college. Or maybe do some home improvement projects. What do you think?" Emily suggested.

"Sweetie pie, you don't have to worry about money, we will be able to get everything you want after I do this one run."

"What run?"

Jacob lied to Emily. "The 5-Sir Company is working on this exclusive deal, and it is confidential. My boss recognized my great driving record and recommended me for the job. I talked with the big bosses, and they said I can't mention the details to anyone. We have to practice the route every Sunday because they don't want anything to go wrong. For the next few weeks, I will be doing my part with the company. I love you, but I can't tell you anything else."

"I'm your wife. You can tell me everything."

"Didn't you hear me say that I can't tell you? Now, woman, get off my back. I tried to have a decent conversation and share it with you. You want more than I can give right now. Please, I am under enough pressure doing this run. I don't need it from you too."

Kimberly walked in. "So, what are you guys arguing about this time?"

Emily shifted her anger from Jacob to Kimberly. "Little girl, stay out of grown folk's business."

"If you didn't talk so loud it wouldn't be everyone's business." Kimberly got something out of the refrigerator, rolled her eyes, and walked out.

Emily was irritated. "Jacob, I swear, I am going to hurt that girl one day. The mouth on her! I would never talk to my mother that way."

"Slow your roll. Pump the brakes. Listen to yourself. She is the child, and you are the adult. Let me be clear."

He stopped dead in his tracks, moved close to her, and looked her dead in the eyes. "I love you to the moon and back, but if you ever hurt a child of mine, you will not live to tell about it. The end! I've got to go to work." He stormed out and slammed the door leaving her wondering what just happened.

She sat down at the kitchen table to collect herself. Reliving the conversation over and over gave her chills and she was becoming afraid of him. The intense look in his eyes burned into her mind. A backup plan was necessary in case Jacob was determined to hurt her. Walking on eggshells when it comes to Kimberly or Jacob was not going to happen.

She called her drug-addicted brother, James. "Hey, how are you doing? Jacob and I just had words, and I think he threatened to kill me. I have never been afraid of him, but I felt a chill when he talked to me."

"Baby Sis, what are you talking about? That man loves you and is taking care of you and those kids. I never liked him. I can smell the bad on him. I knew his reputation in the streets, but he was your choice. Tell me his exact words, what did he say?"

"Here's the story; I was having words with Kimberly with her sassy mouth, and I confided in Jacob that I might hurt her. She brings out so much rage in me that I find it hard to control myself when she goes off. Then Jacob said if I hurt her, he would kill me."

"That's just talk and no action. He would never do that. Trust me, you two will be alright. You will be making sweet love tonight. Girl, are you going to let him hit it?"

"Get your mind out of the gutter, James."

"Sis, seriously, if you ever feel threatened by anyone at any time, just let me know and I will handle the situation. That's why God made brothers. I know I am a registered dope fiend with NA, but I am still connected and can get anything done. That's all I'm going to say about that. We'll chat later."

"Ok, thanks. Bye." After the conversation, Emily felt secure and protected from Jacob. She adored her brother and all his faults.

JACOB/DRAKE

Jacob got a call on his burner phone from Ascension Hospital. Drake was admitted. As Jacob pulled up to the hospital, he counted five police cars with lights flashing and 3 unmarked police cars with officers standing outside the vehicles. His initial thought was they caught Drake and he was handcuffed to the bed like in the movies he had seen on TV.

He did not get out of the car but called Drake to make sure he was not walking into a setup. After all, Jacob knew he was dealing with a crook. And that would be just like Drake to double-cross him.

"Hello man. Is everything OK in the hospital?

Drake struggled to breathe. "I had a severe asthma attack with all the pollen in the air. I'm taking a breathing treatment now. Are you coming to the hospital? I have to tell you something in person."

"I'm here. There are lots of police cars. Do you know what's going on?"

"I heard on the news that two people were shot this morning and were brought to this hospital. The suspected robber is in a room at the end of the hall." Drake paused. "Oh, you thought they were here for me." Then he laughed. "Don't worry; everything is fine in this room. I'm in room 207. If they ask, you are here to see Mr. Oliver." He was using Mr. Oliver even though his last name was Carter.

When Jacob got to the room, Drake was sitting up and taking a breathing treatment. After the treatment, Drake started to talk. "When I had the asthma attack the inhaler was empty. I admitted myself using one of my aliases registered in Arizona."

They talked in code about the 5-Sir run to confirm that they were still on schedule but would not practice this Sunday.

Drake motioned for him to come closer. "I needed you to come to the hospital because I have to give you the key to my hotel room. You must remove the guns and drugs before housekeeping…"

Jacob interrupted him. "What? I am not comfortable handling that stuff and bringing it in the house with my wife and kids."

Drake ignored his protest and continued through his labored breathing. "Everything is in a dark green duffle bag, just take the entire bag. I have another gun in the right pocket of my black leather jacket in the closet."

Jacob reluctantly agreed to this unwise risk. The nurse walked in. She looked familiar. Then it clicked, he saw her at his mother's house for First Sunday Dinner. It was Ivy.

"Hi, I remember you; your name is Ivy, right?"

"Yes, that's right. You are Mrs. Michelle's son. I saw you at her house on Sunday."

"I didn't know you were a nurse."

"I'm not a nurse, I am a patient advocate. I visit the patients to make sure they are being taken care of properly."

Jacob turned to Drake and gave him a handshake and a shoulder bump: "OK, man, I will let you take care of your business, and I will handle that thing." He turned to Ivy and said:"Bye, Ivy, see you on the First Sunday."

Ivy smiled and waved bye to Jacob. She noticed Drake's breathing treatment had medicine remaining. She instructed Drake to finish the breathing treatment. When all of the medication was inhaled, she rang the buzzer for the nurse. The nurse confirmed the treatment was complete and removed the breathing treatment mask. Ivy motioned for Drake to wait until the nurse left and then they would talk.

Ivy enjoyed her job. Before Ken was laid off, they were the perfect match. They were in all the local and national newspapers. Internet posts about them were shared multiple times. Ken was going to be the next mayor, and she was in all of her glory right by his side. She received multiple promotions and was the lead advocator at all the Ascension hospitals in Michigan. Now all she thinks about is getting over, by any means necessary.

She explained to Drake that she was available to advocate on his behalf. She asked if he had any family members she could call. She explained her role was being a problem solver, an inspiration, and a motivator for the patients. Her responsibility was to provide realistic solutions to patients who encounter barriers. Ivy explained that she helps to connect patients with the care that is very much needed. She enjoyed helping to improve the quality of life throughout the community one patient at a time.

When she asked if he had any questions, he said no. Ivy's street smarts kicked in. There was something different about Mr. Oliver. Her instincts told her he was hiding something. She was attracted to him and felt they knew each other or had crossed paths. A little small talk didn't reveal much about him. An emergency contact would tell if he was traveling through, lived in the state, or had a significant other. He had a calm yet undercurrent personality of power and influence, plus he was cute. She checked out his many tattoos and his muscular body. Flirting had no effect. Her efforts were ignored when she reached across him putting her breast close to his face. After getting one-word responses she placed her card on his tray, said her goodbyes, and left. Ivy turned to see if he was watching her walk out.

He was watching that double bounce big but. His tongue circled his lips imagining the taste of her. Drake knew he had to stay focused on the job. This was not the time to get involved with a one-night stand. There will be plenty of time to smash his girl when the job was done. When was sure the nurses were in the shift change meeting preparing for rounds, he took a shower, lathered up, and then pleasured himself in the shower while imagining he was inside Ivy. The shower and orgasm took a lot of energy out of him. When he reached the bed, he used his inhaler and rested well.

KEN/IVY

Ivy was concerned about seeing Jacob at the hospital; she reported to Ken. "Honey, I'm not sure if we have a problem, but I just ran into Jacob. He was here visiting Mr. Oliver."

"I don't know a Mr. Oliver. He is not connected to the family; he might be one of his friends or a coworker. I don't see a concern. Forget about that."

Ken was excited about all of the steps he completed in stealing Mrs. Michelle's identity. Fueled by revenge he set up the website to look like her credit monitoring site. A fake letter and email on the credit monitor's letterhead were sent informing her of a data breach explaining that everything would be corrected after she submitted her information. Ken answered when she called the fake phone number made up in Boole Voice. There is a buyer on the Dark Web Marketplace ready to purchase her information. Everything will be confirmed on the 25th of this month.

"Babe, I have been working nonstop. Holler at your man! What do you think?"

"Sweetheart, you are moving fast. You are doing this thing. I am so proud of you. You rock."

"Thank you, Hon. Don't forget to pick up some dinner on your way home. I have a taste for Italian tonight. Love you. Bye."

Ivy said. "Bye." *Why do I have to always pick up something? All he does is stay at home and play on the computer. I am sick of being the breadwinner, cook, and housekeeper. Is it too much to ask for him to get off of his butt and cook something?*

JACOB

Jacob drove quickly from the hospital to the hotel not knowing when Housekeeping made their rounds. He took the elevator to the second floor. When he got off, he saw a housekeeping cart in the middle of the hall but not near Drake's room. He opened the electronic lock with the key card and quickly entered the room. Luckily the Do Not Disturb sign was on the floor. He quickly put it on the outer door handle. He sat in the chair next to the bed to calm his nerves. As he looked around, the room was neat, and the bed was made. Maybe housekeeping had already cleaned the room. He wanted to get in and out quickly but thought it would be best to wait until housekeeping was off the floor.

He got up and started poking around. There were two duffle bags and one suitcase. He picked up the green duffle bag, which was very heavy, and peeked inside. He saw several guns, two burner phones and what looked like bricks of cocaine, and a brown paper bag. He opened the brown bag and found stacks of cash. *What the Hell?* There was no way he was taking this inside his house. He would leave it in the trunk. Nobody ever looked in his car. He examined the contents in the Black duffle bag. It had two laptops, two iPads, several cell phone chargers, many security cameras doorbells, and two routers. He looked in the suitcase, nothing interesting only clothes.

Toward the back of the closet, hanging up, he found the black leather jacket. He was afraid to reach into the pocket for the gun, he hoped the safety was on and he would not shoot himself. He stopped shaking long enough to reach into the pocket. He got the gun and put it in the green duffel bag. He waited for almost an hour and was sure housekeeping had left the floor. He kept the Do not disturb sign on the door. He pulled his hoody over his head and walked slowly out of the hotel. Jacob carefully put the duffle bag in his trunk. He drove away slowly so he would not attract attention to himself on the security cameras. When he got home, he checked his bank account. Drake had made the initial $10,000 deposit.

KEN/IVY/CHEF

Ivy went to the local Italian restaurant. She caught the eye of the cute muscular thirty-something chef. His biceps were as big as her thighs; his chest looked as hard as a brick. His bald head was smooth and shining. *I would love to rub that bald head.* And his face, *oh my, my, my.* His barber was an artist. The beard was trimmed close to his chin, not straggly, but full and it framed his beautiful, sculpted face. He must be a bodybuilder when he is not cooking. He was Mr. Beautiful. She wished Ken would work out. The only thing Ken did was eat everything in the house. He was proud of his flabby gut.

As she was checking out his biceps and pecs, he caught her staring. With a devilish smile, he gave her a quick wink. She was flustered because she didn't realize he was watching her checking him out. He widened his smile after seeing her reaction to his wink. She turned to leave because of embarrassment but she was next in line. As she started to give her order to the young person behind the counter, he came to the front and motioned that he would take her order. Her legs were wobbly, and her mouth was parched as her brain processed that this handsome man was standing so close to her only separated by the width of the counter.

"May I help you, beautiful?"

She darn near fell over at the sound of his deep bass voice. His eyes were piercing her soul. She felt her coochie jump but she tried to be cool. *You can help me put out this fire between my legs.* "I would like an order of Rigatoni with vodka sauce and a bowl of minestrone."

"Is that an order for one or two?"

Is he asking if I am single? "An order for one please."

"That is what I wanted to hear. May I have your name please?"

Ivy looked confused, should she ask him for his name and number? *Da... it's for the order.* "It's Ivy"

"Ok beautiful Ivy, this will take about ten minutes. Just call me Chef. I will give your order my extra attention, just as I would give you my extra special attention if you were my woman."

Ivy was drawn in by his directness.

Chef leaned his elbows on the counter, looked up at her, and continued in a soft voice: "I would never send you out to pick up anything. You are too precious to be out in the streets alone picking up dinner. I would bring it to you and feed you until you were satisfied. Trust me, I can fill you up. You will be happily pleased. You will be back for more, and I will gladly give it to you."

Ivy felt her coochie jump again, this time she could feel the wetness between her thighs. She knew he was not talking about the food in this restaurant; he was talking about pleasing her sexually. She didn't know what to say, so she just smiled and opened her purse to pay. The chef put his hand over hers and shook his head for her not to pay. When he touched her, it sent a lightning bolt through her body, and she let out a sigh. When she looked at him, Chef had a smile from ear to ear. Embarrassed, Ivy sat down crossed her legs and waited for her order.

He kept looking at her and gave her another wink. When the order was ready, he came from behind the counter and brought it to her. The other workers looked surprised and were whispering to each other, as this was very unusual behavior for him.

"Beautiful Ivy. You used to come here at least once a week, but not alone. Today was the only opportunity I've had to say anything to you. I hope you don't think I was being too forward, but I've imagined this moment for quite some time. I waited for you to come in alone because I would never disrespect another man when he is with a woman even though I have wanted you for a long time. I hope you enjoy your food as much as I enjoyed making it for you. I love great food and I love to eat; my mouth is extraordinary, soft, and sensitive. I can heat it up, serve it up, bring out the natural juices, and then dive in."

He touched her hand, nodded, raised his eyebrows, and walked his sexy body back to the kitchen.

Ivy stood there for a few seconds to collect herself. She and Ken had been there many times, and she never saw him. This was the first time she got a carry-out order. Since she didn't order enough for both of them, she stopped at the local Chinese restaurant and got herself shrimp fried rice and egg drop soup. Ken was napping on the couch and woke up when she came in.

"Hey babe, thanks for picking up dinner"

"You are welcome."

As Ivy opened his bag of food, she noticed a slice of cheesecake with a note attached. She quickly took the note off and put it in her pocket. She explained to Ken that she didn't want Italian, so she got

Chinese for herself. She went into the bathroom to wash her hands and read the note.

Beautiful Ivy, it was a pleasure talking with you, I am the new owner and anytime you are alone, you don't have to pay. Please feel free to use my cell phone number on the back of this note. Enjoy the cheesecake, and dive in. I hope you cum soon. Those words, dive in, made her coochie jump again as she imagined him diving in between her legs. It felt great to have a man notice her and give her compliments with special attention. She felt beautiful, powerful, and sexy. She put the note back in her pocket, washed her hands, and went to the kitchen to eat dinner.

Ken raved about the Rigatoni and vowed they were going back there soon.

GRANDMA

I am sick and tired of all of these computer criminals and data breaches. I'm glad I have the credit monitoring service that takes care of this nonsense for me. Just as the nice man on the phone said, I received the email with the link to handle this. They even offered an extra level of credit monitoring protection. Now that is what I call customer service.

She clicked on the link. Immediately the form populated with her name, address, phone number, and credit monitoring service name.

"This is just what the guy on the phone said would happen. It is not a scam because they have my information." She filled in her social security number, Medicare number, both of her credit cards, and the name of her bank. It also indicated that her stimulus check would be deposited quickly after the form was completed. There was a paragraph asking if she wanted to protect her stocks, 401K, and annuity investments.

"Sure, why not since it's free." So, she meticulously typed in her information, double-checking to make sure all the account numbers were correct.

KEN/IVY

For Ken, the next order of business was to take care of that precious grandson, Cameron, who was dating his younger sister, Bella. Last week Ken made a fake profile, friended Cameron, and got into his account settings. He took over the account and the contacts. This locked out Cameron from seeing and accessing the account. He changed the profile picture to an America's Most Wanted Poster with Cameron's Picture. The next step was to Cyber Bully his friends.

Ken made a fake post calling some of Cameron's contacts losers, hideous looking, and told them they should off themselves. He emphasized that he had new friends and never wanted the current contacts to talk to him in school. He made a global post that Cameron didn't want to be associated with fake friends who are failures with no swag. Ken posted that he caught his sister, Kimberly, having sex in their parent's bed and she got high using their medications. He singled out his sister, Kayla, and said she liked girls and was going to a psychologist because she was twisted and had Attention Deficit Disorder (ADD). He posted pictures of some of Cameron's contacts and called them out by name as backbiters and snitches who should not be trusted. He put a huge X through their picture with a caption saying they were "X'ed" out of this life because nobody wanted to be friends with them. When he completed the posts, Ken took a nap on the couch. He was awakened by the notification of a received email.

"Gotcha, she took the bait." Mrs. Michelle had clicked on the link. Now he had all her information.

He duplicated her email account. All of her incoming emails would bypass her email address and go directly to his. He also duplicated the text message accounts of her and Cameron. Now every text message sent and received would display on his phone as well. Next, he ran up each charge card to its maximum and had the items delivered to a PO Box. The box was created with a fake name and permanent address in Germany which was an empty building that his former investment company lost. He ordered online and went to the electronics store and picked up two 75-inch smart televisions; one for the living room and one for their bedroom at $4,000 each. On the way back from the electronics store, he stopped at the post office and filled out the change of address form. He told the Post office that the entire household would be moving in a few weeks. Since her US mail would be routed to Germany, it would take her months to figure it out and to get her mail.

It was time to do some shopping. Ken bought himself and Ivy shoes from the Chris Lau collection; for her; sneakers for $850 and Kate Trass, for $4,000. For him: Sneakers $1,095, Matellic Loafers $995. That designer purse she wanted, Gucci Ophidia $2,390. Perfume for her Maison Francis for $450, Cologne for him, Creed Les Royals for $1,000, and a few pairs of red bottoms for each of them.

He waited a few days to see if there were any red flags. Ken received an email intended for Mrs. Michelle that showed up in his email account from the first credit card indicating abnormal charges and to respond immediately. He replied to the email and established that there will be a lot of charges and confirmed they would be made by the cardholder.

He logged into her 401K and annuities and then transferred all assets except $100 to an account overseas that was set up using the PO Box as the mailing address.

Ken contacted his partner in crime and sold all of Mrs. Michelle's information to the Dark Web for about $200. Now this family will see how it feels to have their life ruined the way Madison destroyed him. Revenge had such a sweet taste.

After about a week Ken called Social Security to report that she had passed, and they can stop depositing her checks. The Social Security Office said they did not get a notice from a mortuary, or hospital. They asked his name, he said he was her son, Jacob. They appreciated him for informing them before the first of the month when her check would have been deposited.

GRANDMA

Thursday was Senior Citizen Discount Day at most grocery stores. Grandma looked forward to the weekly shopping and chatting with the cashiers. The first stop was the fruit and vegetable market. They always had fresh greens. She got an assortment of turnips, spinach, and kale. She needed ginger root to mix with apple cider vinegar for her feel-good homemade tonic. She grabbed granny smith apples to help with belly bloating. Two bunches of carrots should be enough for this group. She picked bananas that wouldn't go bad quickly. Picking a watermelon with a yellow bottom with bee stings assured her that it would be sweet. Since she had to watch her blood pressure, she used celery sticks for seasoning to eliminate a lot of salt. She could not forget the fresh onions and bulbs of garlic. *My Kayla loves blueberries.* The berries were looking good. She must get lemons to add to the Sweet Tea for her spoiled brother. A five-pound bag of potatoes was more than enough to put in the crock pot with the roast. She pushed her half-full cart to the register.

"How are you today, Angelica?"

"Hi Mrs. Michelle, I am doing fine. Looks like you are planning another great Sunday meal."

"Angelica, you know everyone calls me Grandma. Yes, I am planning my Sunday dinner. I enjoy spending time with my family.

I noticed the ginger was not fresh. When do you expect the next batch?"

"I'm not sure, my guess is the weekend."

The bill came to $60.00, and with the senior discount, it was $50.00. Grandma pulled out her Visa card and tapped it on the machine because Kimberly told her that swiping is outdated. The message came back, rejected.

"I must have done something wrong. I have to get used to tapping this thing and not swiping."

Angelica looked at her with surprise. This never happened to Grandma.

"I will try it again." She got the same error message.

"Mrs. Michelle, I mean Grandma; I'm not supposed to tell you this, but the message on my screen says if I get one more rejection, I have to take your card and cut it up in front of you. You should not try it again. Do you have cash?"

"Oh no, you don't have to take my card, that will not be necessary." She pulled out her American Express card which she only used in emergencies and swiped with confidence. The same thing happened, twice. She quickly tucked her cards back into her purse.

Grandma was extremely embarrassed. "I am so sorry this happened. Angelica, you see, what had happened was... I got a notification that there was a data breach. They must have frozen my card to make sure the identity theft people wouldn't get to my account. The credit monitoring agency is taking care of it as we speak. The next time I shop, there will not be a problem."

Angelica rolled her eyes and her attitude changed because she considered this a made-up excuse. "Do you have cash, or should I have someone restock all of this stuff?"

Grandma was surprised at the change in attitude. She went into her bosom and pulled out her little purse and paid the $50.00. As she was walking slowly out of the store double checking her receipt with her head hanging down trying to figure out what happened, she heard the cashiers talking.

"Girl, I've got a new one for you, the bank froze the card to protect her." They both burst out with laughter.

Grandma was ashamed and felt insignificant because she shopped there frequently and had nice conversations with those very same cashiers. How could she show her face again?

Next, Grandma planned to go to the meat market to buy chicken and a nice roast. The chicken was a staple, but she wanted to surprise them with a roast. She would put it in the crock pot with garlic, carrots, and potatoes. It would cook all morning while they were at church. She could just smell the aroma when everyone came in after service. While driving to the meat market, she remembered the phone call from the nice man at the credit reporting agency telling her about the data breach. Grandma made a mental note to call him again when she got home. She picked up a small roast and two chickens. Grandma paid in cash because she was afraid to use her credit cards again. The bill came to $40, which was all the cash she had left. She made plans to go to the ATM the next day, and then finish shopping.

When Grandma got home, she pulled out the letter and called the nice man from the credit reporting agency. She explained everything that happened at the fruit and vegetable market.

Ken answered using his business voice, "Ma'am I am so sorry that happened. Please accept my apology for not telling you we had disabled your credit card. According to my records, we mailed you another card. You should receive it on Monday."

Grandma was relieved. She had enough cash stashed in her house to carry her until Monday. Her social security check will be deposited in a few days.

CAMERON

Kimberly stormed into the kitchen while Cameron was eating breakfast. She yanked him up by his shirt and twirled him around. She put him in a headlock and started pounding his face. He was taught not to hit girls, so he tried to get her off of him. He was blind-sided. He screamed for her to stop while trying to pry her arms from around his neck.

"Cameron, I will kill you for what you did. How could you? I hate you!"

Their mom, Emily, came in to break them up. She immediately yanked Kimberly off Cameron. She flung Kimberly across the kitchen like she was a rag doll. Kimberly hit the wall with a loud thump and slid down. She hit her head and was dizzy for a few seconds. When she came to herself, she looked at her mother with so much hate. If her eyes could burn, her mother would be a crisp potato chip. She wanted to kill her mother. Kimberly stood up and started walking briskly toward her. Jacob walked in.

"What the hell is going on in here?"

Emily quickly responded, "I came in just in time. This smart-mouth Kimberly was pounding Cameron for no reason."

Full of anger, Kimberly shot back. "For no reason mom? For no reason? Is that why you threw me against the wall? As usual, you don't know what you are talking about. Cameron is posting lies about our family on social media. He said I had sex in your bed."

Jacob checked his wife. "Emily, we will talk later. Son, did you do that?"

Kimberly shouted, "Yes he did!"

Cameron matched her shouting voice. "No, I didn't. I have not been on social media for several days."

Kimberly handed her phone to her father. "Here dad, look at this!"

"Son, this came from your page. What is the matter with you? I taught you better than that. Let's look at some of the other posts. Why are you saying this about your sisters? She is not doing drugs and there is no way a daughter of mine is gay. Cameron this is bad."

"Mom, Dad, you've got to believe me. I must have been hacked."

Emily finally broke the death gaze on Kimberly. She addressed Cameron, "Can you go on social media and delete these posts?"

"Ok, I will do it right now in front of everyone." Cameron feverishly tried to log in to his social media account. "Wait, I am locked out of my account. Someone has hijacked my account and pretending to be me. I saw this happen on the TV show Tech Talk. I have no control."

Jacob, Emily, and Cameron cautiously walked over to Kimberly and everyone looked at Cameron's phone.

Cameron said, "The only way to circumvent this is for Kimberly and Kayla to post that this is not me and to ignore these posts."

Kimberly physically took several steps back, stood in an unyielding stance tall like a soldier, then crossed arms her arms, and locked threatening eyes with Cameron: "I am not convinced you didn't do this. I know we've been beefing for a few days. Maybe this is your way of getting back at me. Mom, you've made it obvious that I am not your favorite person. Maybe the two of you conspired to ruin me?"

Jacob tried to establish peace. "Kimberly, stop it. This is your brother and your mother you are talking about. Baby girl, we will get to the bottom of this, I promise you."

Later that night Kayla came in late from school. Kimberly asked her if she saw the mean posts from Cameron.

"Yes, I saw the posts and I refuse to speak to Cameron. I will not stay in any room with either of you."

"Why are you mad at me? I didn't do anything. You should confront him and make him explain himself."

"What's the use, he will deny it. There will be a fight and nothing gets resolved. Cameron is dead to me."

"I talked to him with mom and dad. He said someone hijacked his account and is making up stuff, and it's not him."

"I don't care! Cameron is plutoed, like the planet, non-existent to me. I am not like you. Just leave me alone. I am preserving my peace because it is clear to me that all I have is me. You guys don't care about me, please go away."

The girls parted and went to their separate rooms and slammed the doors.

CAMERON/GRANDMA

Cameron popped in to see his Grandma. He was upset. He rang the doorbell; she peeked through the curtains and opened the door.

"Baby, what's wrong? Are you in trouble? Get in here."

"I don't know what's going on Grandma. Someone has hijacked my social media account and said terrible things about Kimberly and Kayla. They think it's me. Kimberly and I got in a terrible fistfight. Mom and dad are taking her side. My friends are sending me text messages saying they don't want to be friends anymore and to watch my back. Everyone hates me." His face became twisted while trying not to become emotional.

Grandma responded, "I have not been on social media for a few weeks, so I wouldn't know anything about that. This is terrible; I think the world is going crazy. Baby, did you hit your sister during this fight?"

"No Ma'am, I tried to get her off, and then mom came in and separated us. She had hulk-like strength when she pulled Kimberly off me. And then, she threw her against the wall."

"She did what? I told Emily how to handle Kimberly. Is she OK?"

"She is fine but does not believe me. I keep telling her that I didn't write those things. Kayla refuses to talk to me and treats me like I'm invisible."

Grandma took a deep breath. "Is there a way for you to delete the account?"

He explained that it had been hijacked and what that means.

"Do you think your girlfriend Bella did something?"

"No, I don't think she is smart enough to hijack an account, but I would not put it past her to try it."

"Can you contact the social media customer service department and tell them to shut it down?"

"They don't have a phone number because everything is done online. I have been locked out of my account. If I can convince Kimberly, Kayla, and my best friend that it's not me, they can contact the Admins of Social Media, and then they can shut it down."

"Maybe you are a victim of the data breach?"

"What data breach? What are you talking about?"

"I didn't want to concern you all with my problems. I received a letter in the mail telling me about the data breach. And that many people have been affected. I followed the directions in the letter, and it is being corrected as we speak.

Grandma smiled and expanded out her chest. "I even signed up for the free extra credit monitoring. They said they would send me an email. As instructed in the email, I clicked the link. It took me to the website. I filled out all of the forms and now I am protected from the bad guys. Maybe, I can refer you to my data breach people? They might be able to help with your social media account. I had a little problem yesterday. My credit cards were rejected. I called the credit monitoring service, and they are fixing the problem."

"Let me see that letter." He read it. "Grandma, this is a scam. Notice that there is no return address on the letter. I'll bet there was not a return address on the envelope either. I heard about it scam on the Tech Talk show."

"No baby, I talked to the company, and they told me they were aware of what's going on. They are correcting the data breach issue and will send me a different credit card on Monday."

"Don't tell me you called the phone number in the letter."

"Yes, what other number would I call? I know how to take care of my business. I've been taking care of myself long before you were born."

"Grandma, go to your files and let me see something that your credit monitoring company mailed you a few months ago." Cameron looked at the phone number on each document. They were different. His heart sank. "Grandma, tell me, what information did you put on that website's form?"

"I answered all the questions about my social security, Medicare, credit cards, and banking. I wanted the extra protection on everything."

Immediately Cameron called the phone number on the fraud letter. The office was closed because it was after hours. "Grandma, you have a big problem. Tomorrow morning, we are going to the bank to check on your accounts. We will call the credit card companies using the phone number on your cards, not the phone number on this letter. I've got to go now. I didn't tell mom I was leaving the house. Lord knows I'm in enough trouble. I need to do more research for you. I will start with the Tech Talk webpage. They are the most reliable source for these scammers. Before I go, Grandma, will you get a prayer through and ask God to talk to Kimberly, Kayla, and my best friend?"

"Yes, baby, I will say a prayer for you. Remember, you can pray to God yourself. Grandma won't be here forever, and you need to know the power of prayer." She hugged Cameron and prayed while they hugged.

"Heavenly Father, my grandson is experiencing a
lot of stress about the social media account.
I ask that you soften the hearts of his sisters and his friend.
Dear Lord, please bring to light those
responsible for this awful thing.
God, assure him that everything will work out for his good.
Father, please restore peace in their house.
We rebuke the devil and all of his schemes.
No weapon formed against them will prosper.
In your son Jesus' name we pray. Amen. "

The next day, Friday, Cameron left school early to take his grandmother to the bank. The cashier informed them that the account only had $100. All the money was transferred as she instructed them.

Grandma was noticeably angry. "I didn't ask anyone to transfer money or close any accounts."

They called the branch manager. He escorted Cameron and Grandma to an enclosed office.

"Ma'am, here is the email you sent. The second email confirmed it using the new phone number you left with us."

"No, I didn't. Somebody needs to call the police." She started getting loud asking for the police. "Cameron, call 911 right now because there has been a crime."

Cameron touched his grandmother on the shoulder. "Grandma, let him finish."

The bank manager continued. "It seems we have a bigger problem. May I see your ID please?"

"I've been coming here for thirty years, everyone knows me. Greg, and you know me. What is the problem?"

He sternly replied, "Three pieces of ID please."

She went into her purse and showed him her driver's license, Medicare card, and Library card. She slammed them on the desk "Here, is that good enough for you?"

"Ma'am, according to our records, you passed away last week and the executor of your account, your son, had the money transferred as your final request."

"My son! I don't believe it. My only son has done this to me. Wait until I get a hold of his narrow behind."

"Grandma, calm down, remember your blood pressure. I'm sure Dad didn't do this. It was probably the scammers."

"I forgot about that. You are probably right." She turned to the bank manager "How do I fix this because as you can see, I am very much alive?"

"It's not that easy. I am sure this has affected your social security check and your Medicare benefits. If you get sick and need to go to the hospital, you might be denied services or have to pay a huge amount. You will have to contact all of these agencies and prove your identity. In the meantime, I will start an investigation to trace where your money was electronically sent.”

“Can you do me one favor, under the table? For my sanity's sake, please check my son's account and tell me if there has been a hefty deposit lately.”

“You know I can't do that. But I just might leave the screen open while I step out of the office for a quick second.” Then the branch manager left the office.

Grandma squinted her eyes to look at the screen. “I can't believe your father recently had a $10,000 deposit to his account. I am going to kill him. Cameron, drive me to your house so I can kill your Dad.”

“Grandma, my gut feeling is that Dad didn't do this. It was the scammers who pretended to be him, and they are the ones who said you died and are causing the problems.”

Cameron shook hands with Greg, the branch manager. They said their goodbyes and then left the bank.

When they arrived at the house, Jacob was about to leave for an overtime shift.

Grandma walked up to him and got in his face. “Jacob, my only son, tell me what's going on.”

Jacob stopped like he had received an electrical shock thinking she found out about the job with Drake involving the 5-Sir company. “What are you talking about Ma?”

“Don't play with me boy, I know all about the money.”

“Ma, come on, you know what? I have to get to work.”

“Ok since you want to play dumb. Someone has stolen my identity, they did something with my credit cards and took all my money from the bank including savings, checking, stocks, 401K, and my annuity. Do you know who did that, Jacob?"

Jacob was relieved that she was not talking about the deal with Drake. "Ma, do you think I would do something like that to you?"

"I didn't think so until the bank manager told me my son called to say I was deceased, and my son said to transfer the money out of my account. I only have $100 to my name."

"No way, I didn't do that."

"Well, son I want to believe you. Just explain one thing." She took a pregnant pause for a dramatic effect. "Where did the $10,000 deposit come from that was put into your account a few days ago?"

Jacob had to think fast. He couldn't tell her that Drake gave it to him for the job. "That was a loan from work. I got an advance which is a low-interest loan so I could fix up the house for Emily. I haven't told her yet, it's a surprise for our anniversary."

Cameron was relieved his father was in the clear. "See Grandma, I told you. Dad didn't do it."

She said, "This whole thing is making me tired. Son, after Cameron takes me home, he will fill you in on the data breach that has taken over my life."

Cameron drove Grandma home. "Grandma, let me see that letter again. The data breach company should be open because it is normal office hours." He called the number. It was disconnected. He took a picture of the letter.

Grandma was distraught. "My life is ruined. I don't know what to do. I am so brainless. How could I not recognize this as a scam? Am I too out of touch with reality to take care of my own business?

Are you guys going to put me in a nursing home because I am so stupid?"

"You are not stupid, and you are never going to a nursing home. We will figure this out. Don't worry."

Cameron called the local police to make the report. The same two officers came to the house. The black officer who she called Officer Muscle Man and the Asian officer who was slightly overweight who she called Officer Donut Lover.

Officer Muscle man spoke. "Well, Ma'am, here we are again. What seems to be the problem?"

"You two again? Are you the only officers in the precinct?"

"No, we are assigned to this block. It's part of the City's effort to make the police familiar with the neighborhood and its residents. When the weather warms up, we will be walking in the streets meeting and greeting everyone. The purpose is to form a team so the residents and the police will work together."

Grandma went into great detail about the credit cards, the letter, and the bank. Cameron filled in the parts she glossed over.

Officer Donut Lover took pictures of the fraud letter and copied the official phone number from her real credit monitoring service. "We will get back to you with a case number. We have agencies that specialize in correcting problems such as these. The case number is vital when contacting resources to re-establish that you are living. The police department has an excellent Intelligence Team. They will chase your money and catch the perps. I suggest you immediately call the credit card companies using the number on your cards and say that your cards have been stolen."

When the officers left, she and Cameron called the phone number on the back of the Visa card. After being on hold for half an hour, a friendly and perky agent answered. Grandma gave the agent the card number. Immediately the friendly agent turned into a nasty and sarcastic tyrant.

"Who am I speaking to?"

"This is Mrs. Michelle?

"Please answer the following questions. Can you provide your address, the last four of your social security number, and your security question?"

Grandma provided the requested information.

"You've answered all of the questions; however, our records indicate the cardholder is deceased. We will go after the estate for the thousands that were charged using the credit card."

"Listen to yourself, I am not deceased. I have been a victim of identity theft. My card has been stolen, and I don't want to allow any more purchases."

The agent replied with a snide attitude, "You don't have to worry about that. The card has reached the maximum."

Grandma was stunned. "No, you don't understand, it was not me. The last time I used the card was a couple of weeks ago at the gas station for $20.00."

"So, you are telling me, there are $15,000 of fraudulent charges."

"Yes, that is exactly what I am telling you."

"Have you filed a police report and reported this to the credit reporting agencies?"

"Little girl, yes! Today, we filed a police report. I am going to call the credit reporting agencies Monday morning because they are closed now."

The agent was irritated by her little girl remark. "When you receive the case number from the police and the credit reporting agencies, then call us back. We will remove the charges after our research department has verified your case numbers. If that is all, have a nice day." The agent disconnected the call.

Grandma was noticeably upset. Cameron comforted her until she was calm again. "Grandma, we have to call the American Express folks too."

She was surprised at how much Cameron knew about the identity breach and what to do. *These kids come into this world holding electronics.* She was glad he did the research and was helping her: "I can't take much more being treated like a criminal. I am exhausted but I will make the call if you think I should."

An agent answered immediately. Grandma explained about the identity theft and the police report case number.

The agent responded, "Ma'am, we sent you an email asking about these substantial purchases. Here is the email where you replied confirming the purchases were yours."

"No, I didn't. I never received an email. My identity was stolen and someone is pretending to be me."

"I want to believe you, but I am looking at several emails sent and received. Let me go to another screen to verify a few things. Our records indicate the cardholder is deceased. Hold on, let me get my manager."

"Cameron, I don't know how much more of this I can take."

Finally, the agent returned to the call. "I need to confirm your identity. Please answer these questions, your date of birth, the last four of your social security number, and your security question."

"Here we go again," Grandma answered the questions.

"Ma'am, our records indicate you passed away last week after the purchases were made. That sounds suspicious to me."

"I am not dead, but my identity has been stolen. Will you please stop purchases from being made and shut down the card?"

"No problem, the card was shut down because the maximum of $20,000 was reached."

"I cannot believe this," Grandma grumbled.

The agent tried to free her from worry; "I think I know what's going on. This happened to four of my previous callers. Did you receive a letter asking you to go to a website and fill in your information for additional credit card monitoring?"

"Yes, yes, I did. Finally, someone understands. I thought it was the right thing to do."

The agent explained. "There was a special blog on social media instructing people how to steal an identity. In addition, the blog also showed the thieves the steps to take to cover their tracks. It was featured on the TV show Tech Talk. In that same show, they cautioned the viewers about what to look for and not to respond to these letters."

"I didn't see that show and now I am messed up."

"Don't worry, I've flagged your account. I will have our Internet Technical Specialists research all of the purchases. We will find this person. Also, after the investigation, we will not hold you liable for the purchases."

"Thank you so much." Grandma turned to Cameron, "Did I forget anything?"

"Who are you talking to?"

Grandma began her monologue. "I'm talking to my grandson; he is helping me unravel this whole thing. I'm a senior citizen and this is taking a toll. Why do they target the elderly? When they are caught, jail time should be doubled for offenses against senior citizens and children. I'm tired of being sick and tired."

"Mm-hmm. Is there anything else I can do for you?"

"No that's all. Thank you very much."

"Ma'am, have a wonderful day, and we will be in touch. Goodbye."

Grandma turned to her caring grandson, "Cameron, I am tired. My head is hurting, my bones are aching, and I have no energy. I feel like a useless soiled dish rag. I am going to cancel the First Sunday dinner. There is no way I can cook and enjoy you guys. I need Saturday to relax and calm myself. Please tell the family we will get together next month. Hopefully, everything would have cleared up by then. I will call my brother tomorrow so he can make plans to pick up something for himself. Tell your dad, that I am still mentally capable of taking care of my affairs and that I don't need to go to a nursing home because I did this absurd thing. I feel so dumb."

"Grandma, you are the smartest woman I know. This is one thing that we will fix. How many times do I have to tell you, that you are not going to a nursing home, and that you are not dumb? You need to tell Jesus about this. Isn't praying your thing? See you later."

CAMERON/KAYLA

When Cameron got home from helping his grandmother, he sent a group text to his sisters and his best friend again explaining that he was hacked and locked out of all of his social media accounts. Kimberly and his friend responded to say they would think about it. He looked up and Kayla was standing at his bedroom door. Kayla was still struggling with how to come out to her family. She swallowed her pride and mustered up enough courage to confront her brother. Did he recognize that she was different from the boy-crazy girls? Did he tell anyone? Are people talking about her behind her back? She wanted to know.

"Cam, how did you know?"

"Know what?"

"That I like girls."

"Whoever made up that post said that I didn't!" He paused, turned his head to the side, and squinted his eyes. "Wait a minute… Are you telling me you do like girls and you are gay?" He tried not to look shocked or judgmental.

"Yes, that is what I am telling you. Your post forced me to think about coming out. I'm not okay with this. I am asking you to take it down because I am not ready for the world to know. So, I guess I am coming out to you personally. You and Grandma are the only ones I've told. Please don't tell anyone until I am comfortable telling people myself. Trust me; it will not be a social media post." She was hoping Cameron considered her feelings; she searched his face for a sign of acceptance or rejection. He was difficult to read.

As Cameron processed what he heard he shifted his body from side to side trying to figure out what to say so he would not offend her. He had too many thoughts at the same time. His words came out like an interrogation. "Wow, this is information overload. How did this happen? When did you figure this out? Is Nancy your girlfriend? I knew she acted kind of Butch. Oh, I don't want to offend you, is Butch an acceptable word?

Kayla looked at him wondering. Still, she was not sure if he accepted her news or not. There was an awkward silence while she stood with her head down feeling alone and detached.

Finally, Cameron spoke; "Kay, I need some time to wrap my mind around this. I will be supportive of your choices. You know I didn't write that stuff about you being gay, on drugs, and the other stuff?"

"Yes, Cam, I believe you now."

"Cool, can you post a message on social media explaining that my account has been hacked, hijacked, and cloned, and these remarks are not coming from me?"

"Don't worry, consider it done. Please keep my secret until I'm ready to tell mom and dad. I know Dad will hit the ceiling."

"You've got that right. He hates anything that might look gay. Good luck with that."

KEN/IVY

Since Ken cloned Cameron's phone, he saw the text message Cameron sent to his sisters and best friend. Ken immediately got on social media and said they were imposters pretending to know him. He called them social media trolls and asked everyone to delete their messages and block their accounts.

Kimberly fired back directly at Ken and said, "You are the imposter. If you are my brother, what is my Grandfather's nickname?" When Ken did not answer, Kimberly wrote, "As everyone can see, this is the imposter, not my brother. Please ignore any posts from him and unfriend this jerk. We will report him to the administration so they can trace the account back to the hijacker and officially delete the account. Thank you, everyone."

Although their Grandfather died before they met him, he was affectionately referred to as "Dude" because he was chilled like that. Grandma said it was for the cool in him.

FRIDAY
JACOB/DRAKE

Drake was released from the hospital and took a taxi to his hotel room. He called Jacob and they finalized the plans. "Man, thanks for picking up the duffle bag. Bring it back today when you get off work."

"Sure. I was wondering, why do you need laptops, cameras, drugs, and guns? I didn't sign up for all of this. Anyway, are you physically competent to do this since you just got out of the hospital? You might have an asthma attack in the middle of this whole thing."

"Jacob, I guess you looked through my stuff when you were just supposed to pick up the green bag. I understand but I told you about the gun. I'm a nice guy so I'll give the laptops as an extra thank-you gift to the guys taking care of the surveillance cameras. The extra doorbell cameras are anonymous gifts to the businesses and homes of the ones that we trashed. Listen, all you need to know is that I will do my part. You just do yours. And about my health, I am ready. Like I said, just let me quarterback this and we will be rich. Tomorrow is D-day. We are going to do this thing! Everything is in place. The plane is ready to take the vaccine to the motherland. Everyone has been using their burner phones. Let me remind you again, do not call me using your personal cell phone, continue to use the burner phone.

After the job, throw the burner phone in the lake. By the way, you never said thank you for the deposit I made. You see, I got your back, my brother."

"OK, see you around nine tonight when I get off work."

Jacob got off work and went to see Drake. He arrived at Drake's hotel at nine fifteen. He noticed three guys hanging around outside the hotel. He put on his gangster look, his pimp walk, and a threatening face. He looked them in the eye to let them know he was aware of their presence and that if they tried to rob him, he was not the one.

When Jacob came into Drake's room, Drake checked his watch and frowned at the fifteen-minute difference. He gave Drake the duffel bag and told him the gun is in the bag. They went over the plans one last time and Jacob felt more confident about the robbery tomorrow.

When Jacob left, the three guys were still standing around the entrance. He looked at them and kept walking. As he drove off, he checked his rearview mirror and noticed that they had entered the hotel.

Drake responded to the knock on his hotel room door. "Hey guys, come on in. Did anyone see you?"

They responded no. Drake gave them the laptops and extra cameras. He instructed them to keep the burner phones on them at all times and when the product was on the plane, to throw their phones in the Lake before they drive across the bridge to Canada.

While Jacob was driving home, he called his mother. She was flustered.

JACOB/GRANDMA

"**H**ey Ma, how are you doing?"

"I am terrible. I know we talked briefly about this earlier. I want to give you an update. My Identity breach is much worse than I expected. But there is no need to be overly concerned because I am still great at managing my affairs. I will fix this."

"I know you can manage your affairs. Why did you say that?"

"I don't know… just saying. Anyway, This horrible situation gets worse every minute. Cameron has been my rock. He has a first-class head on his shoulders for such a young guy."

Jacob responded, "I can't believe this! Our family seems to be cursed. First the social media thing with Cameron; and now, someone has gone after you. This grinds me. I am pissed off at the highest level of pisstivity. Why do hackers usually target senior citizens? OK Ma, I'm coming over right now. You tell me everything when I get there. I will handle this. I will find out who did it and they will pay dearly."

"Slow down son, you sound like a street vigilante out for revenge."

"You dam right. They tried to hurt you, and I will hurt them. That is not a threat or a promise, it's a guarantee."

"Jacob, stop all of that crazy talk. The police will get to the bottom of this, and everything will come out in the wash. You calm down. I need you to be calm so I can stay calm. Honey, I want to say again; I'm sorry I accused you of taking the money out of my account, please forgive me. Cameron knows everything he will fill you in. I am going to take a long bath and go to bed. Promise me, no more of this street justice talk."

"OK Ma, goodnight."

She said a quick prayer before going to bed:

Dear God, I don't know what's going on.

I always try to do the right thing,

but it seems like I've done the wrong thing

and allowed the bad guys to take over my identity.

I ask that you keep my mind strong and alert

so I don't make these mistakes again.

I don't want to go to a nursing home.

Lord, you know who did this.

Was I a random person, or was I targeted?

I don't understand who would want to do this to me.

Give me strength, direction, and discernment please Lord.

I feel my blood pressure rising and I am getting anxious.

I don't want to have a stroke.

I ask that you sturdy my mind and my heart.

Calm down my nerves so I will have a restful and peaceful night.

Allow my thoughts and my body to relax

and float into a deep sleep

as I am cradled in your hands.

In your son Jesus' name I pray, Amen.

She put on sleep meditation music, placed lavender essential oil in the diffuser, and drifted off to sleep.

JACOB/CAMERON/I.T. GUY

Jacob called Cameron, "Son when I get home, I want to hear every detail about what's going on with your grandmother."

Cameron told his dad everything again in great detail. He said it was hard to see his grandma perplexed and she had no energy when dealing with the credit card folks. Her spark was gone, and it made him sad.

Jacob was very upset and smoked a couple of cigarettes outside to calm down. He contacted a friend from the community college who was an IT expert. They talked at length about what happened. The IT guy told Jacob that her information was probably sold on the Dark Web Marketplace, and they can expect a lot of crazy things to happen. Jacob gave him Grandma's email address, phone number, Medicare number, and Social Media Account. After about two hours he called back.

"Man, I hope you don't mind but I hacked into your mother's email and saw the emails that were sent to her and supposedly sent from her. Just as I suspected; her information has passed through probably hundreds of buyers. It's usually a snowball effect where her information is sold over and over again. The good news is that I executed a program that encrypted her IP address and redirected the thread with her identity to a dead end. That stopped it from going further down the rabbit hole. I am not sure how many places purchased it. However, the damage has been done. And the news keeps on coming. I'm doing an automatic reverse IP search to find the computer that initiated this theft. The program has been running for about an hour and is still cranking away. When it is done, I can tell you the exact address where it originated. I can also tell you who has been reading her email and sending emails pretending to be her. The program should be done in the morning. Oh man, I love technology. I just texted you a list of agencies and phone numbers she can contact to get everything reversed. The banks, credit card folks, and even the police will take months to follow up and catch these guys. Don't worry, these places I gave you are legitimate agencies. I'll text you tomorrow with the results."

"Thanks, man, how much do I owe you?"

"This was fun. I'll hit you up another time. As long as you owe me, I will never be broke! Peace."

SATURDAY MORNING JACOB/IT GUY/DRAKE.

Jacob was getting ready for work. The timing was everything. It was drilled into his head that he has to pull out of the building at 2:15 pm. He was very nervous because the nine months of planning has come to a head. But Jacob needed to make a stop before going in, so he left home early. While driving, he got a phone call from the IT guy.

"Man, I have an IP address that hacked into your mother's computer and stole her Identification. They live in a little area called The Village. I advise you not to go there. You don't know if it is a company or if it's a home with shady individuals. If you decide to call the police with the IP Address, don't tell them you got it from me. Some of my methods are not standard practice." He chuckled.

Jacob was feeling his inner Thug. "Thank you, man. I don't need the police to take care of this, I can handle it. If I didn't have an important task at work today, I would go over there right now. Later I will link up with some of my homeboys in the hood on Mack and Bewick and we will visit them. How dare they think they could do this to my mother? Wait, I've got another call coming in; I'll catch you later. Much Love and thanks again." Jacob hung up his personal phone and picked up the burner phone.

He knew it was Drake; "OK, Jacob. Are you on time for what we have to do? Remember, you get in your truck and pull out at exactly 2:15 pm. The traffic lights are set to be green until you get to the transfer point then it will be red for the specified time. The cameras are set, and the vital ones have been disabled. Everyone is ready. How are you doing my man?" Drake coughed.

Jacob started feeling uneasy about Drake's health. He could be back in the hospital hooked up to a breathing treatment while everything is going down. "The question is, how are you doing? Is your breathing OK? Do we need to reschedule this?"

"What are you talking about? With all the work I've put into this, of course, I'm ready. Don't punk out on me now. If you do, there will be consequences to pay and it won't be pretty."

Jacob felt disrespected. "I know you are not threatening me. You need to take some of that bass out of your voice when you talk to me."

"Hold on soldier, why are you being so sensitive?"

"Sorry, I'm a little on edge. My mother had her identity stolen and I know where they are. I want to shoot up the place and then burn it down."

Drake recognized that Jacob was sparling out of control and not concentrating on the day's job. "Stop right there, get your head in the game, and stay focused. You have nothing to do today except this job. I need you to be laser-focused. You can worry about your mother after the job is done. Now, let's go over the timing again."

They went over it from start to finish. Drake said very jubilantly, "Alright, here we come, the new millionaires!" Then he coughed uncontrollably and took a long drag from his inhaler.

SATURDAY MORNING
JACOB/GRANDMA

As Jacob left the house, he gave Emily a peck on the cheek. When he got in his car, he texted his mother the contacts provided by the IT guy. He stressed the importance of making sure she had the police report's case number. He told her that the ones who stole her identity lived in The Village. He asked if she knew anyone who lived in that area and that he was going to the Village to find them.

She does not like texting, so she called him, "Son, don't do anything, let it go and let the police take care of it. I can't recall any of my friends living in The Village."

"I can't let it go, Ma. If they mess with you, they mess with me. Nope, I'm not having it. I will get my boys and we will make a house call. Got to go now, I'm pulling up at work. I have fifteen minutes to get my truck and do my job. I love you Ma. Bye."

"Do not go to The Village, let the police handle it. I got another call coming in. Bye".

SATURDAY MORNING GRANDMA/ROY

Grandma got a phone call from her brother, Roy. She told him, she was not going to put up with his foolishness today because she was going through some serious stuff. She noticed her brother's voice was faint and he was gasping for air. Roy said he had fallen and was in terrible pain. His voice started to shake. He explained the paramedics were there and were taking him to Ascension hospital. Roy asked Grandma to go by his house to lock the door and close the blinds. She had only seen him emotional once and that was when their mother died. She assured him she would come to the hospital after she left his house.

Grandma called Jacob. The phone went to voice mail. She knew he was at work and couldn't answer the phone while driving, so she left him a voicemail about Roy. She called Emily and informed her where the paramedics were taking Roy. Grandma took a quick wash-up, ran the comb through her hair, and said a prayer before leaving:

Dear God, please let my brother be alright.
I know he is a pain in the butt, but I love him.
Dear Lord, please don't let his hip be broken
because so many seniors don't recover
or recover very slowly from this break.

I don't want to put him in a nursing home.
God, I am trusting in you
and putting my faith in you that everything will be alright.
And God, I am going to break a few
speeding laws getting to my brother,
so please keep the police away from me,
and give me traveling grace, thank you.
In your son Jesus' name I pray, amen.

Grandma arrived at Roy's house. The door was closed but not locked. She went inside and it was a mess. It looked like he had not tidied up in months. There were newspapers on the floor, dishes in the sink, and on every kitchen surface. Clothes were scattered all over the living room and in the bedroom. My goodness, what was that smell? The carpet smelled like grimy feet. Grandma moved the clothes in the living room into one pile in the corner so she could walk around. Then she put all the dishes in the sink. She soaked them in water, dish soap, and bleach. She would deal with it later.

Grandma went into the bedroom and removed the clothes from the bed and floor and put them in a pile in the corner so she could create a walking path. Then she discovered six brand new knee braces. She went into the bathroom and gathered his toiletries, toothbrush, and toothpaste. She grabbed Roy's medicines off the counter and put them in a paper bag. Just before leaving she sprayed air freshener throughout the house, closed the blinds, set the burglar alarm, locked up, and left. She was in and out in thirty minutes. Grandma stopped at a fast-food restaurant to get herself a snack and a big cup of sweet tea for Roy.

SATURDAY AFTERNOON
JACOB

Jacob walked into work as usual. He punched his timecard and spoke to everyone. He double-checked the clock on the wall with his watch. It was synced to the second. He was assigned truck number 512. Jacob looked at the mechanic's repair sheet. There were no problems with the truck. Protocol mandated that he logged in to the Electronic Truck Driver's Work Diary when he got in the truck. Jacob verified that the planned route and drop-off location was accurate and were the same as usual. He was moving quickly and was two minutes ahead of schedule. He got into the cab and noticed everyone was watching him. Usually, he got there and departed as soon as possible. But everything depended on him exiting at 2:15 pm and doing the speed limit. Finally, it was time for him to pull out of the garage. His friend ran up the cab and started a conversation. "Man, we are having a party tonight. Do you want to fall through?"

After Jacob listened for a few seconds he interrupted, "That sounds good. I will pass it by my wife. I'll call you later."

That short conversation took about thirty seconds. He was still in good shape if he did the speed limit. He drove out and turned off of Rochester Road, then made his usual left turn onto Adams. Jacob was so nervous that his stomach made him nauseated. The thought of him being shot and beaten up was too much. He started dry heaving and tried hard not to throw up. He let down the windows and stuck his head out. He took out his burner phone. He started to call Drake to tell him he couldn't do this because he was too nervous. He disconnected the call before it started to ring. He looked up and noticed the light was yellow. He must have slowed down when he stuck his head out the window. He plowed through the yellow light to stay on schedule. In two more blocks, he would arrive at the rendezvous. His personal cell phone rang. It was his son, Cameron.

"Hey Dad, just checking on you, I'm getting a bad vibe today."

"Don't be silly, I'm fine. It's your grandmother you should be checking on. She was upset when I talked to her earlier today. Give her a call. Got to go son, I love you."

Jacob hung up before his voice started shaking which would have given him away. He was terrified about what was about to happen. Also, he knew his son had a gift of discernment. He thought Cameron could hear his heart beating because he could feel it vibrating through his body. It sounded like his heart was beating through the speakers in the cab. He didn't want to answer any questions. His hands were sweating. He wiped them on his pants.

As Jacob got closer to the meeting place, he made the planned slight turn which the GPS did not register as off route. He saw the transfer truck. He drove up to the red light. He saw three men wearing ski masks jump out of the truck. His gut told him they were the same three guys at Drake's hotel the other night. One of the guys shot out the front tire. Jacob motioned to them that the plan is for him to call work to report a flat tire first and for them to keep still.

Jacob used the in-dash phone to call his manager, "Hey, I believe I ran into an enormous pothole, or I hit something. It feels like one of my tires is damaged. I wanted to let you know I am leaving the cab to check it out."

"Turn up the volume, keep the phone active and leave the door open so I can hear everything as you exit the truck," the dispatcher instructed.

Oops, this was not in the plan. Jacob acted as if he didn't hear him. "You're breaking up. I'm not sure what you said, but I will call you after I check it out." He disconnected the phone call. One of the men used an explosive to open the trailer. The three men moved quickly and transferred the vaccine to the waiting truck. Jacob had a bad feeling and became suspicious of them. Three minutes passed and his company phone rang on the dashboard of the truck. Almost simultaneously, his personal cell phone rang. It was his mother. He did not answer either call.

The guys finished loading the truck in the planned four minutes. They put a bag over Jacob's head. When they punched him in the stomach, he doubled over and groaned with pain. They pistol-whipped him on his head and in his face. Since he could not see the blows coming, the pain was unexpected and was nothing like he had ever experienced in his street fighting days. Then, they shot him in the upper right chest. He felt a burst of excruciating pain.

Oh no! Drake said they were going to shoot me in the arm. Jacob felt like he was moving in slow motion. He could feel the warm blood coming out of his chest. He wobbled toward the truck for leverage to remain standing. The force was too great. As Jacob fell, his legs were like jelly. He felt his knees buckling. He hit the ground like he was shot out of a cannon. His butt hit the ground first, and then his back. He heard his back crack and thought it was broken. Jacob's instincts kicked in and he knew to bring his chin to his chest to protect his head. The burner phone fell out of his pocket and slid under a rear tire. Jacob looked down as the bright red blood filled his shirt. The warm blood started running down his pants. The pain was burning and agonizing.

Jacob could hear the three men talking. "That is one less check we have to split." They removed the bag from his head, laughed, and drove away, leaving him to bleed out. Jacob was in critical condition. He felt himself slipping away.

Meanwhile, Cameron kept getting intense feelings about his dad. Even though his dad assured him that he was fine, Cameron couldn't shake the feeling. He needed to hear his dad's voice again before a fun day with his friends.

The ringing of Jacob's cell phone jolted him awake. Luckily, it was in his pocket on the left side that was not affected by the gunshot.

"I've been shot and robbed," Jacob yelled into the phone.

Stunned Cameron responded, "Dad, what's happening?

"Son, call the police and my job. Let them know I've been shot. Use conference calling so you can stay on the phone with me."

Cameron called the 5-Sir Company and asked them to use the truck's GPS to get his dad's location. They knew exactly where he was. The company called 911, and the police. They could hear Jacob breathing hard. The 5-Sir Company assured Cameron that help was on the way.

They told Jacob to hang on. Jacob's energy was drained. Warm sticky blood covered his shirt. Jacob was tired and wanted to take a nap. His breathing became slow and shallow. Cameron kept talking to his dad, telling him everything will be alright and to stay awake. Jacob responded with grunts of un-hum and an occasional OK. Cameron was shaking and pacing while encouraging his dad. He knew dad's life depended on him. He kept thinking that his voice might be the last thing his dad heard.

Cameron heard the sirens through the phone. He told his dad, to perk up and listen for the sirens and to hang on because they were near. In seconds, the police were there. They were followed by an ambulance and a fire truck. Bringing up the rear were two security cars from the 5-Sir Company.

The paramedics sprinted to Jacob. Cameron could hear everything going on. They applied pressure to stop the bleeding. Since blood was still coming out of the hole, they increased the pressure and the blood stopped. Jacob moaned from the excruciating pressure on his chest. Next, they dressed the wound to help the blood clot. Then, they applied the tourniquet. As the paramedics pulled the tourniquet tighter and tighter, the pressure increased, and the pain amplified exponentially. To prevent Jacob's lungs from collapsing, they wrapped the chest with plastic to keep air from being sucked into his chest. Finally, the paramedics quickly found a vein and hooked Jacob to an IV. When he was transferred from the ground to the gurney there was a big agonizing bump. The paramedics talked to Jacob to keep him awake. Jacob's phone was not to his ear, but he was holding it on his side.

"Who are you talking to?" they asked.

"My son." Jacob was gasping for air and his breathing became labored.

"We're taking your phone," the paramedic explained.

"Dad, Dad, don't die. Dad, talk to me!" Cameron pleaded.

The paramedic informed Cameron, "We are taking him to Ascension Hospital. We are hanging up so we can continue to work on him."

The phone went silent. Cameron was shocked and tried to remember what his dad told him to do. He was motionless for a few moments. He started running home to tell his mother what had happened. He was only 17 and dealing with two adult situations. His grandmother relied on him to help her solve her stolen identity. His father might be dying, and he had to keep him talking. And to top everything off, now he had to tell the rest of the family what was going on. He didn't know who to call first, his mom or his grandmother. He stopped running and decided to call his mother.

Emily was shocked. She screamed out of frustration. Cameron's social media hack Grandma's identity theft, Uncle Roy in the hospital, and now her husband. What else could go wrong? She called Kimberly and Kayla from their rooms. She told Cameron she would pick him up at the bus stop on their way to the hospital. The ride was full of questions. Kimberly demanded that her mother tell her everything about her father's condition. Emily kept her cool but could feel her blood boiling because of the way Kimberly addressed her. All Emily knew was what Cameron told her; he was shot and robbed, and the ambulance was taking him to the hospital. Kayla went to a peaceful place in her mind to block out the thought of her dad dying. When Cameron got into the car, the barrage of questions began again. He told them he could hear their dad moaning and groaning with pain. He explained how he could hear the paramedics working to keep him alive. Emily listened but didn't comment. She was anxious about her husband but had to be strong for her children. It would be horrible if she got into a car accident on the way to the hospital. She had to stay calm.

The ride in the ambulance was very bumpy. Jacob felt every turn, thump, and pothole. He was getting light-headed and starting to drift off to sleep.

"Stay awake if you want to live," the paramedics instructed Jacob.

Jacob answered questions about the day's date and the president's name. When the ambulance reached the hospital, they moved him quickly to the waiting bed in the emergency room. The paramedics transferred him to the bed. Jacob felt unbearable pain during the transfer and almost fainted. They kept telling him to stay awake and kept talking to them. A doctor examined his chest wound, then poked, and prodded his stomach. They turned him on his side to look for an exit wound. Since there was no exit wound, they knew the bullet was still inside. They had to move fast. Then, the doctor addressed the gashes on his head and face from the pistol-whipping. The doctor gave directions to take him immediately to an operating room.

SATURDAY AFTERNOON
GRANDMA/ROY/JACOB

In a rush to see her brother, Grandma parked next to the ambulances at the Emergency entrance. She had to wait half an hour because there were lots of police cars surrounding an ambulance. She was instructed to stay back or go to another parking lot. Finally, Grandma was able to enter. She rushed to the counter and asked about Roy. They directed her to a bed in the ER patient room. The curtain was drawn, and she slowly pulled it back. "Roy, are you OK?" She walked over and hugged her brother.

Roy was in agony. He opened his eyes and gave her a closed-mouth smile. He was glad to see her. He was on oxygen. She asked the nurse if he could have the sweet tea. She said yes. Roy sat up and drank the sweet tea.

After being with Roy for about an hour, the doctor came in. "Nice to meet you, ma'am. The nurse told me you were here. I have reviewed the chart and your brother's hip is broken in a couple of places. His bones are not as resilient as they should be. If the fall had resulted in a minor fracture, we could use nonsurgical treatments like compression and exercise. But since his hip is broken and he has osteoarthritis, he will need a complete hip replacement."

Roy had friends who had hip replacements and never recovered. His best friend was in a nursing home for five years after his hip replacement, then he died. Roy had delayed having hip replacement surgery because he didn't want to become a burden or lose his independence. This was terrible news. Roy felt sad and hopeless.

Grandma assured her brother. "Don't worry, Roy. I will take care of you. It will be alright. Doctor, how soon will you schedule the surgery?"

The doctor explained that he would let Roy rest for two days so the swelling could go down. On the third day, they would do the replacement. Roy would have to stay in the hospital for a few days after the surgery. He would be in the hospital for five or six days if all went well. The doctor encouraged Grandma to make sure Roy's hospitalization and other medical information were in order. He said to contact Medicare and make sure Roy received all the benefits he was entitled. Roy was eligible for a walker, cane, elevated toilet seat, in-home physical therapy, home nurse visits, transportation to and from doctor visits, and housekeeping.

Roy didn't have any questions. Grandma thanked the doctor as he left.

Grandma's cell phone rang. It was Cameron. "Hi baby, did your mother tell you about your Uncle Roy?"

"No Grandma, I'm calling to tell you about my dad. He was shot and robbed while driving the truck today."

"What! Jesus, Joseph, and Mary, what is going on? Oh no, not my baby. Where is he? Where is my son?"

Roy was concerned about his sister and sat up in his bed. "What is it? What happened to Jacob?"

Grandma is anxious. "Oh, dear God. I feel like Job in the Bible when complete devastation happened to him at the same time. Lord, please have mercy. Jesus, Jesus, Jesus! Cameron, where did they take him?"

"They took him to Ascension."

"What? That is where I am with Roy. I am in the emergency room until a room becomes available."

"I'm with mom and the girls and we are on our way there," Cameron replied.

"Ok, bye." Grandma grabbed her purse and rushed out of Roy's room. She went to the nurse's station in the center of the emergency room. As she approached the nurse's station, she noticed there was only one nurse on duty. She was on her cell phone and looking at her computer screen. Then, a second nurse came to the desk and started working on her computer. Neither of them acknowledged Grandma who was standing directly in front of them. She was done being polite and wanted answers.

"Excuse me. I understand my son was brought here because he was shot. May I see Jacob, please?"

The two nurses looked at each other with a side-eye. "And who are you?"

"I am his mother."

"Ma'am, I thought you were with the other gentleman, and you said he was your brother."

They got on the phone and called the lead nurse. When the lead nurse arrived the other nurses told her everything that was said.

Grandma was glad someone in authority was listening to her and that she would see her son soon.

The lead nurse told the others to call security because she suspected this lady was wandering around the hospital looking for patients.

Grandma was growing more frustrated. "Now you wait a minute, young lady. Roy is my brother, and now I am concerned about my son who was brought here with a gunshot wound."

"Please calm down ma'am. May we see some ID please?"

She showed them her driver's license. The lead nurse was on the computer for about two minutes.

"You have a different address from both patients, Jacob and Roy. Please wait here while I cross-reference their records to see if you show up as an emergency contact." Grandma waited at the nurse's station for what seemed like an eternity.

As she was waiting, Emily entered with the grandchildren. The girls were upset, and Cameron was trying to be strong. When the lead nurse returned, Emily pulled the children close to her as Grandma spoke to them. Emily looked anxious because she remembered the conversation she had with her brother James. She thought James followed Jacob and tried to kill him for threatening her.

"Ma'am, you are on the record as Roy's contact, but not on the list for Jacob's contact. I'm sorry, but we can't tell you anything about the other patients in the hospital."

Grandma went off. "I don't give a rat's ass what that damn record says. I am his mother and I demand to know where my son is and what's going on with him!"

Cameron, Kimberly, and Kayla looked at each other and in unison said, "Grandma cussed."

Grandma was in rare form. "I ain't been saved all my life. If they don't tell me about my child…"

Emily cut her off. "I am Emily, Jacob's wife and I'm his emergency contact. I am verifying that she is his mother. You have my permission to tell all of us what's going on with my husband." Emily showed her driver's license, and the nurse changed her attitude.

Grandma looked sorrowfully and apologized to the nurses. "I am sorry for my language and attitude. If you are a mother, I am sure you understand my frustration about my son." She looked at the grandkids and Emily: "I am so sorry. I lost control; will you all please forgive me?"

The grandkids looked at each other, smiled, and nodded. They thought it was cool hearing their Grandma cuss. About ten minutes later, the nurse asked everyone to leave the general waiting area and go to a private conference room.

Immediately, Grandma started whaling. She retreated and pulled away and started to sink to the floor.

Cameron was trying to hold her up. "Grandma, what's wrong?" She became limp. Her body language reminded Cameron of a toddler he saw having a fit and falling out in a department store.

Grandma shrieked, "No, no, no, not the private room! Not my son, I don't want to hear it. I am not going to the private room."

Emily was confused, "Grandma, it will be ok. They just want to talk to us."

"No, that is not true. Oh, God no, not my son. The last time I was asked to go to a private room to talk to the doctors, they told me my mother was dead. That is why they have a private room; so the families can grieve in private. I am not going to the private room for them to tell me my son is dead. No, no, no. I don't want to hear it. No, not my son. I am not going in that room."

The grandkids looked puzzled and exchanged glances. Grandma was always the sturdy rock of the family. They had never seen her like this. She always comforted them and now the rock was crumbling.

Roy heard her voice; she was upset. He was concerned about his sister. She needed him. He tried to get out of bed. The bed alarms sounded and the nurses rush in and saw him trying to get out of bed.

"Don't you dare try to get out of bed," the nurses yelled at Roy. They looked at the monitors and his blood pressure was 200/150 and his pulse was 200bpm.

Roy shouted, "I have to help my sister. Something is wrong."

"If you don't calm down, we will put restraints on you. We will check on your sister and let you know what's going on." They gave him a shot to mildly sedate him.

Meanwhile, another group of nurses was trying to calm Grandma. "Your son is not dead, only injured. The family is being escorted to a private room because the doctor didn't want to discuss his condition in the general waiting area within earshot of the other families."

Grandma gathered herself, wiped her tears, and calmed down. She followed the family and walked silently into the private room. She took a seat and looked like the rock that she was - unmovable, brave, majestic, and she was prepared for the news.

The doctor explained, "Jacob has a gunshot wound to the chest." Emily fainted. Kimberly and Kayla screamed. Cameron tried to catch his mother who was not a slim woman. The doctor called a nurse.

Grandma didn't move, she acted like she didn't see or hear the commotion. She was unphased she was as hard and stoic as a brick statue. She said in a calm voice, "Tell me everything about my son."

The doctor waited until the nurses revived Emily. They took her vitals and gave her a bottle of water. The children were hugging each other, rocking, and were calm again.

The doctor continued, "The bullet entered the soft fleshy tissue of his upper chest near the collar bone. It didn't hit any organs or bones. Jacob was very lucky. He is being prepped for surgery and we will remove the bullet. If there are no complications, he can go home in a few days. He will need extensive physical therapy. In addition, he suffered a few blows to his head and face that were stitched up. The brain CAT Scan showed no inflammation or concussions."

Everyone was relieved. Emily went to the restroom. While there, she called her brother.

"James, tell me you didn't do it," Emily pleaded.

"I didn't do it. What are we talking about, Sis? I didn't do what?"

"Jacob was shot in the chest today. Somebody tried to kill him. Did you do it?"

"Hell no! I didn't do it. If you want me to put out some feelers on the street to see who did, I can do that. But Baby Sis, my hands are clean. I had nothing to do with it. How is he doing? Is he going to survive a shot to the chest?"

"The doctor said he was lucky, and he is going to make a full recovery. No, don't put any feelers on the street. We will talk later." At that moment, she vowed to never tell her brother anything that went on between her and her husband.

LAW ENFORCEMENT/ THE 5-SIR COMPANY

When the family came out of the private room there were lots of police. A couple of guys had on FBI jackets and there were two men from the 5-Sir Company. They asked the nurse about Jacob's status. Then they turned to the family for answers.

Emily took the lead, "My husband is being prepped for surgery. The doctor said it was a flesh wound in his upper chest near his shoulder and collarbone. What do you want with him?"

They didn't answer her question but asked if anyone had talked to him today.

Grandma went into great detail. "Yes, I talked to my son today. You see sir, my identity was stolen and I think the people who stole my identification were the ones who shot my child. Jacob was very angry and wanted to find them. He told me they lived in The Village. He didn't give me a street address, but he gave me the IP address. If you find that street address, you will find who shot my son. They probably followed him. You know he drives the same route every Saturday."

Cameron was next. "I talked to him when he was driving, and he was fine. Then I called back a few minutes later, and he told me he had been shot."

The 5-Sir Company spokesman was stern and looked at everyone like a suspect. "We will get to the bottom of this. Thank you." He then turned to the other law enforcement officers. They huddled together to discuss and compare facts. The vaccine was missing. A tire on the truck was shot out. It looked like they were waiting for him, or it was an inside job. A phone that was probably dropped during the robbery was discovered. While the truck was in tow, the phone was crushed, but they will ask the police to dust it for fingerprints. The IT staff at the 5-Sir Company will try to save the motherboard on the phone. Since the drivers take the same route, they were an easy target. The cameras will be checked from the city, private homes, and local businesses.

The family traded shocked expressions. Grandma asked, "What would the identity theft people want with a truck of vaccines?"

The police asked everyone to stay put because it might be necessary to question everyone separately. Emily insisted on being present when her children were questioned.

An ATF agent rushed into the hospital. "I need to know the whereabouts and status of Jacob."

Grandma quickly went into Mama Bear mode. "That's my son. What do you want with him?" He brushed her off and waved his hand like she was insignificant as if to say *whatever*. The grandkids looked with wide eyes waiting on Grandma to cuss again. The AFT agent huddled with the other law enforcement officers, and they all left without saying another word.

THE GETAWAY

The thieves were jubilant about the first part of their heist. The distance to the airport was only twenty minutes and they would be Scott-free. They joked about killing Jacob and getting his share of the money. Since they had on ski masks, he couldn't identify them if he lived. All the cameras were disabled, so there was no proof.

Drake called his fellow thieves in the transfer truck to make sure they were on schedule. They said, "Yes, in a few minutes, we will roll up to the airport."

Drake had an ID card indicating he was ground crew at the airport. The getaway plane was in the designated hanger. He approached them to make sure everyone was comfortable. He started working his PR magic. He recognized one of the guys as a previous business associate. "Hi guys, we are right on schedule. Everything is going according to the plan."

The truck pulled up to the gate. Drake directed them to the hangar. Before he gave the order to unload, he asked for proof that the money was transferred. Drake checked his account on his tablet. He gave one of the guys a bag of cocaine and told him it was a gift for doing business with him on this project. The three transfer guys said they wanted proof the money is in their accounts. Drake did not plan on making the transfer at that exact moment. He told them when they are finished loading, it would be in their accounts. Drake watched as each box was loaded on the plane at lightning speed. After the last box, he pressed the send button, and their money was transferred. He reminded them where to drive the transfer truck into the lake. The keys and a fresh car were waiting for them at that same spot. They checked their accounts and drove off.

When they arrived at the lake, they tried to drive the truck in the lake, but it kept getting stuck in the mud. The thieves found a long branch to press on the gas, but the tires kept spinning and getting deeper into the mud. They decided since they had their money and the key to the car to go across the border, the truck was not their concern. They wiped away every fingerprint inside and outside of the truck. They removed anything that connected them to the truck.

Drake watched as the plane ascended. He walked slowly off the tarmac, through the building, and to his ride-share car. It was finished, and he was rich! He went back to his hotel room and called the hospital to check on Jacob. "Hello, I am inquiring about the status of my friend Jacob."

"I am sorry sir. We cannot give out any information," the nice operator responded.

"I understand, darling. But will you let him know, Mr. Oliver, called?" Drake hung up the phone and took a deep breath to savor his victory. Now it was time to transfer the remainder of Jacob's money. He imagined the joy on Jacob's face when he looked at this account.

There was a hard knock on Drake's door. It was the same AFT officer who rushed into the hospital. He was accompanied by the FBI and the local police. They took the burner cell phone directly out of his hand. The ATF officer announced, "You are under arrest for drug trafficking and suspicion of murder. We have warrants from

Michigan, California, and Mexico. Drake, you are a slippery one. We knew you were in the State, but not sure where you were until we got a tip this morning."

Drake responded, "Cut the chatter. I don't have to answer any questions. I know the drill." They handcuffed him and placed him in a police car. They searched his room and removed several items including the two duffel bags.

At the station, all of the questions were regarding the drugs Drake brought over the State line from California. They wanted his sources and operation locations. They knew about one of the drop-off locations in California. After five hours of interrogation about drugs, Drake didn't say a word and was not shaken or stirred. The officers left the room. Drake knew he was going back to the pen and didn't want to lose his life while serving time. If he snitched on his sources or customers, he was a dead man walking. Drake kept his head down. He was surprised there were no questions regarding the vaccine. He pulled off the great Motherland save and couldn't brag about it.

CONFRONTATION

While Roy was knocked out from the sedative, and Jacob was undergoing a 7-hour surgery, the family went to the cafeteria. When they walked into the hospital cafeteria, they saw Cameron's friend Bella eating lunch with Ivy and a man who they assumed to be her husband. He was very handsome with bulging muscles and a shiny bald head. They were talking and laughing.

Cameron approached Bella. "I knew you two were friends before you came to my grandmother's house. Why did you pretend not to know each other?"

Bella was bothered by Cameron. "Get over it and me. I don't owe you an explanation."

Of course, Kimberly could not be left out of any kind of confrontation. "I told you! She is a hoe, a thot, a hooker, or whatever you want to call this tramp. She has thousands of provocative pictures on the internet and social media. She is just nasty. I heard that her phone number is on the boy's restroom wall to call for any kind of sex. She has an Only Fans page with XXX-rated porn. I'll bet she has V.D. with her dirty smelly self. Well, how about that, Bella the Baller?"

Bella rolled her eyes.

Kimberly was out of control, "Come on girl! We can go toe to toe, especially if you messed with my grandmother. Make your move, and we can throw down right now. I will slap the taste out of your mouth."

Grandma touched Kimberly's shoulder to calm her down.

Cameron expressed his disappointment with Bella. "Yes, I saw those pictures. She is not who she pretends to be."

Grandma was still trying to get a rational answer from them. "You both owe me an explanation. Bella, I don't know your story, but you are not looking good right now. Ivy, I trusted you because you said you were my daughter's friend. I had a feeling you were up to something when you kept going to the bathroom. Did you go into my closed-door office?"

Ivy started lying her butt off. "No, why would I do that? Why would you think I was in your office?"

"Yes, I think you did. I have my reasons. Who are you? Did you take anything? I can call the police and turn you in. I have one more question… I'm curious; what part of town do you live in?"

"I don't see what that has to do with anything," Ivy turned up her nose and whipped her hair around. "But I live in The Village".

Grandma smiled. "Ok, I was just curious. Bye for now. You girls enjoy your lunch."

Grandma kept her cool because she'd just confirmed who stole her identity. She motioned to everyone to leave them alone. They sat on the opposite side of the cafeteria. Kimberly still had her eyes locked on Bella, ready for a fight.

After the confrontation, the man kissed Ivy on the cheek. "We'll talk later, beautiful."

"Ok, Chef." He left the cafeteria and did not look back.

JACOB

The family went back to the emergency room waiting area. The nurse gave them Jacob's room number. A police officer was guarding the door. Only two family members could visit at one time. The nurses invited Grandma and Emily to go in first. Jacob was still groggy but awake. There were lots of monitors and drainage tubes. His nasal oxygen tube was halfway out of his nose. Emily took a step back and caught her footing. Grandma was tall and solid as she walked to her son. She fixed the oxygen tube and kissed his forehead. She saw the gashes on his head and face. She laid her hand on his forehead and prayed:

"Most gracious heavenly Father,
thank you for sparing my son's life.
It is nothing but your grace that kept him.
Dear God, I know you have your hand on him
and his angels are protecting him.
I am in awe of how you spared him
with a chest wound and head trauma.
I thank you and give you all the praise.
Don't let anyone come into this room who will do him harm.
Only allow the hospital staff
who will do their job to the best of their ability and glorify you.

Lord, I repent for losing my temper
and using profanity, please forgive me.
And don't let my grandchildren think less of me.
Lord, please keep your protective eye on my son. Amen."

She left the room. Grandma simply needed to lay eyes on her son and touch him, then she was fine.

She told the grandchildren to wait. She knew their mother needed extra time with her husband. They kept saying, Grandma cussed, and then they laughed. When Emily came out of the room, she prepared her children for the way their father looked. They assured her they could handle it and wanted to see him. They went in together. Kayla stayed back and stared. She was traumatized and too scared to move. Kimberly went right up to him and kissed his forehead, gave him a big smile, and said "Dad, you will be OK."

Cameron was relieved that his dad was alive but was overcome with emotion thinking about what might have happened. "Dad, when I talked to you, I was so afraid. I knew your life depended on me. I called for help as quickly as I could. Dad, I don't know what I would do if you had died." Kimberly and Kayla hugged him.

Jacob waved for his son to come closer, and he held his hand. "It's OK son, you did the right thing. I will be alright. I am very proud of you. Thank you for saving my life."

The nurse came in and announced they should let Jacob rest and come back tomorrow. Everyone left his room. They found Roy's room and went to visit him. Jacob was on the 5th floor and Roy was moved from the emergency room waiting area to the 4th floor. Roy was awake but a little drowsy.

Grandma questioned the nurse, "Why is my brother tied to the bed?"

"He kept trying to get up to see what was going on with your family."

She leaned down and whispered in Roy's ear. "My dear brother, Jacob was shot, and they robbed his work truck. He had surgery and they removed the bullet. He is going to be fine. He is on the 5th floor and you are on the 4th floor. Please do not try to visit him. Now rest and do what these people tell you. I am tired, and I am going home. I see you finished your sweet tea. I guess you know, there will not be a first Sunday dinner tomorrow." She put her hand on his forehead and prayed.

Most gracious heavenly father, thank you for my brother,
please watch over him as he
sleeps and prepares for surgery.
Restore his strength.
I am asking for an extra measure of your grace.
Please put it in his mind that he has to obey the nurses.
In your son Jesus' name I pray, Amen.

Kayla tried to encourage her Uncle Roy. "When we come to visit tomorrow, I will bring the chess game. If you are up to it, we can play a quick game."

"Of course, Kayla. I can whip your butt again."

Everyone shared a laugh and then left.

GRANDMA

Cameron drove Grandma home, and Emily followed. "Grandma, I had a feeling something was going to happen to Dad. I could feel it in my bones."

Again, she explained his gift, "You are emphatic, and you can feel others' feelings. You know what they are thinking and can sense when they are not telling the truth. God has given you the gift of discernment and prophecy. You must always listen to God's still voice. You probably saved your dad's life."

When Emily drove up, he hugged grandma and got in the car with his mom and sisters. Grandma waved bye to everyone.

As soon as Grandma opened the door, her house phone started ringing. She ran to answer thinking it was the hospital regarding her son or her brother. It was a spam caller talking about a knee brace and repeating her Medicare number. She slammed the phone down. Exhausted, she put on her night clothes, said a quick prayer, and fell asleep.

GRANDMA /JACOB

Grandma called the police and told them she had an idea of who stole her identity. The offer assigned to her case would not be in until Monday, so she left a voice mail message. Since it was not her Sunday to count money after church, she decided to skip church.

She called the Pastor and told him about Jacob and Roy and added them to the prayer list. She didn't go into detail because the rumor mill at church runs rapidly and hard. There were so many "feet that run swift with mischief."

She needed some *me time* before going to the hospital. Grandma knew she would spend most of the day at the hospital going between the two rooms. She put her packed lunch in a lunch bag cooler. She didn't want to run into Ivy or that other girl in the cafeteria.

Grandma checked on Jacob first. As she walked into the room, one police officer approached her. Jacob told him that she was his mother and the officer stepped back. There were two police officers in the room. They seemed very friendly and left so he could have private time with his mother. Emily called to check on Jacob. He told her he would call her back when his mother left.

"Son, tell me everything that's going on," She said in a low concerned voice.

"The officers are assigned to stay outside the room until the next shift arrives. They fear that the ones who shot me will come back and finish the job. There is a possibility that the robbers think I am dead."

"Oh my God, this sounds like a movie. Son, do you feel safe in here? Do you want to come to my house? You know I have that .45"

There was a news flash on the TV: *The 5-Sir Company was robbed of the vaccine plus booster solution. One of their employees was shot in the chest and taken to a local hospital. The status of the employee's condition is undetermined but feared fatal.*

Jacob explained to his mother, "The 5-Sir Company told me they had to tell the press something. My name or condition will not be disclosed."

Grandma finally got up enough nerve to pull back the sheet to see Jacob's bandages. She got woozy and stumbled backward in a chair after seeing the drainage tubes. It made her sick to know they had to drill a hole into his side to drain the fluid. The chest tube was connected to a closed chest drainage system, which allowed air or fluid to be drained and prevented air or fluid from entering the pleural space. The system was airtight to prevent the inflow of atmospheric pressure. She sat back and collected herself and started asking questions.

"Did you see the guys who shot you? Did you know them? Is your boss going to fire you because of the robbery? Are you under investigation? Talk to me son, what's going on?

Jacob knew he had to monitor his words, so he didn't give away the plan with Drake. He explained that he didn't see the guys who shot him and that it happened so fast that he didn't have time to react. He said when he got out to see what happened to his tire, they put a bag over his head and shot him. While he was on the ground, he explained that he could hear the robbers opening the truck and getting the vaccine.

Jacob started to drift in and out of consciousness as he was telling the story.

"Son, I am sorry for talking so much. Now, get some rest. I will be back after I go check on my brother." She walked past the officers, smiled, waved, and asked them to take good care of her son. They nodded.

GRANDMA/ROY

Grandma stopped at the cafeteria and got Roy a tall sweet tea. She moved quickly and did not look around because she didn't want to run into Ivy. She walked into Roy's room.

"Good morning old man, how are you doing?"

"Who are you calling old? I see you got me some sweet tea. In that case, you are looking beautiful today, Sis."

"I thought so."

They both chuckled.

Roy was concerned about his nephew. "How is Jacob doing? I was watching the news and they said he might be dead."

"He's not dead, but he did get shot in the chest. There are police officers outside his room. Enough about him, how are you doing?"

"I promised those sweet nurses that I would not get out of the bed if they took the restraints off."

He proudly displayed his free wrists. "Like all the good patients, I press the button when I need to go to the restroom. They get me out of bed twice a day to walk around so the hip does not freeze up. The surgery is scheduled for tomorrow at 10:00 am." He looked like a sad puppy. "Will you be here when they take me to the operating room, sis?"

"Of course, I'll be there." Grandma's cell phone rang three times. Thinking it was either the nosy church folks or some spam callers, she sent each call straight to voice mail.

"You know that cute girl you invited to Sunday Dinner, she works here. She came into my room and asked if I needed anything. She's a Patient Advocate."

Grandma started to feel anger towards Ivy. "Don't talk to her! She is the one who stole my identity. That girl looked at my papers in my office and now I am having all kinds of problems."

"Sis, are you sure? She was friendly. We talked for about an hour. I told her about Jacob and everything. I didn't know anything about someone stealing your identity."

"It's OK. Don't worry. Everything will come out in the wash. By the way dear brother, I will tidy up your filthy house so you can get around with a walker, but after that, we are going to hire you a housekeeper. You have to be able to take care of yourself, so you don't go to a nursing home."

"Hell to the new! Ain't nobody sending me to a nursing home. I know my house is a mess. I will do better, I promise."

Roy's hospital roommate was snoring very loudly. Roy fanaticized about putting a pillow over his head. When he was not snoring, he was farting, and sometimes he did both.

Grandma sat with Roy for about an hour, then left to make one last check on Jacob. He was asleep, so she didn't disturb him.

On Monday morning, Grandma got up at 6:30 AM, did her Bible reading, and said her prayers.

"Dear God, thank you for waking me up this morning.

Lord, I thank you for sparing my child
and taking care of my brother.
I ask that you keep your arms of protection around my family.
God, I know you are everywhere, and I cannot send you anywhere,
but I am asking for special grace and mercy for my brother, Roy,
as he goes through his hip surgery today.
Give me the strength to be supportive of him and Jacob too.
I don't understand everything that's
going on with Jacob, but you do.
Please give him favor so he can return to his job.
In your son's Jesus' name, I pray, Amen."

Grandma took a quick shower and had breakfast. Oatmeal with walnuts, blueberries, and raisins will keep her full all morning. She packed lunch and put it in her lunch cooler. After getting dressed, she called the police station to get the case number for her complaint. Then she gave them additional information about the IP Address in The Village belonging to Ivy. However, she didn't have the house address. At 8:00 am, she called the phone numbers Jacob's IT guy sent her to establish she was not dead. The folks who answered the phone were very understanding and knew how to get her identity back. It's good that Jacob had friends who could help her. She had not heard from the police, the real credit monitoring company, the credit card companies, or the bank.

Her first stop was to see Jacob. As she walked past the officers, she waved and said hi. Another officer was talking to Jacob and taking notes. The officer handed Jacob back his phone. She wondered what he was doing with it. When she walked in and spoke, the officer excused himself and told Jacob they would be in touch.

He sat up, turned up the television, and started eating his breakfast. She was pleased he was showing signs of recovery and was looking better.

"Baby, your uncle is having his hip surgery today and I have to be with him before they put him under, or he will have a fit. So, I will come back while he is in surgery."

"I understand Ma. I will be alright. Yesterday, I texted you the IP address of the computer located in the Village that stole your identification. Did you get it?

"Yes, I got it. Thank you."

"Now, I am going to text you the actual house address in the Village. After talking with my wife, I decided to listen to you and let the police take care of this. Please pass all of this information to the police."

"OK, son."

"Ma, Don't worry about me today. Emily took the day off and will spend it with me while the kids are in school."

She kissed her son on the forehead and went to Roy's room. When she walked in, his bed is not made, and he was not in his room. Her heart moved to her stomach. Did something happen during the night? Did they already take him to surgery? Had she missed being there? She rushed to the nurse's station. "Excuse me; I am looking for my brother Roy. He was in room 403. He is scheduled for surgery at 10:00 am. He is not in his room. Where is he?"

"He was moved to a different room because there was a heated altercation with the roommate."

Grandma shook her head as she walked toward Roy's new room. When she arrived, Roy was talking to the nurses. They were going over the procedure again.

"Hey baby sis, glad you made it."

The nurse was impatient. "Sir, please lay still."

The doctor arrived. He asked if there were any questions. Then, he marked his hip to make sure they got the correct one. The nurses kept asking Roy questions about how he was feeling. "We are going to give you something to make you relax."

Roy was animated, "Oh, here comes the good stuff."

Everyone laughed. In less than a minute, he was out like a light. She barely made it in time for him to know she was there before he went under.

"That was quick! I thought they didn't knock you out until you were in the operating room," she questioned the nurses.

"We always give the mild sedative while the patient is in the room, so the patient does not get nervous on the way to the operating room. He gets the anesthesia in the operating room. The surgery will take about two hours. Plan to see him in about three or four hours after recovery."

While waiting in Roy's room, Grandma made another phone call to the police. She told them that she had a private investigator trace where the email theft originated. She verified that the IP address was given to the officer. Next, she gave them the house address in the village that Jacob's IT guy gave him. The officer said he would look into it but would need more proof. She told them, that was the proof, and to go to that address.

KEN /IVY

s Ivy was driving home from work, she called Ken. "Babe, did you know Jacob is in the hospital along with Mrs. Michelle's brother Roy?"

"What happened, was it a car accident?"

"No, there were two separate incidences. The older guy broke his hip and Jacob was shot in the chest. You know what? I don't believe the family has any idea that it was us who ruined their life. The old man talked for an hour and didn't mention anything."

Ken felt good about himself and asked her to pick up more Italian food for dinner. He sat back in his recliner and logged into his laptop. The Internet was acting strange, and the Wi-Fi was buffering. He checked the connections, and they were secure. Since he didn't have a reliable Internet connection he decided to do something to keep busy.

Ken reflected on the things Ivy said about pulling his weight around the house. She was right and he was determined to do better and let her know how much he appreciated her. He washed the dishes and cleaned the kitchen. He had no idea how to run the washer. He sorted the clothes in piles of white, dark, and towels. He emptied the change and paper from their pockets. There was a receipt from the Italian Restaurant in Ivy's pants pocket. He thought it was strange that she didn't put it with the rest of the receipts. He placed it on the desk. He picked up the stuff on the floor and ran the vacuum in the bedroom the living room and the dining room. Since it was easier than sweeping, he vacuumed the kitchen too, and then he mopped it. This was a lot of work. He could see why Ivy was complaining. This clean house should make her happy.

JACOB/IT GUY

The IT guy was concerned that Jacob went to the address in The Village. He was agonizing about giving Jacob the information and if it was the right thing to do. He knew Jacob was hot-headed and irrational at times. He called Jacob to check on him and make sure he didn't give his name to the police.

"Hello, man. I heard you got shot. Did you go to the house in the Village? I told you not to go over there. Have you lost your mind? What happened Jacob?"

"No man, I didn't go there. I got shot during a work thing. Someone robbed my truck and shot me in the chest. I will be OK."

"That's jacked up. Who wants the vaccine? It's free everywhere. That does not make sense. Very few people survive being shot in the chest. Somebody's looking out for you."

"You got that right! My mother prays for me all of the time. Prayer is her thing.

The IT guy confessed, "I don't believe in God or prayers. I believe in the universe and technology. When you are dead, you are done, the end. Heaven and hell are on this earth, I'm glad you are going to be OK. Did your mother give the police the IP address and the house address in the Village?"

"What do you mean you don't believe in God? I am sure it was God using you to gather the evidence to help my mother. And I know for sure it was my mother's prayers to God that saved my life. OK, man, you do you. We will talk about this later. I've got to go, my wife is here now. Thanks again for the information and for checking on me."

IVY/KEN/GRANDMA

Ivy came home from working overtime. Ken asked about the food. She said she was too fatigued and forgot to pick it up. He was disappointed and starving. She knew the routine but didn't seem interested in what he was going to eat. They argued again about dinner. Secretly, she stopped by to see the Chef and was not thinking about Ken.

In the heat of their argument, Ivy didn't notice that Ken cleaned the house and vacuumed.

Ken lit into her. "You had one job to do - pick up dinner. Now, what are we going to eat?"

"I already ate. Why didn't you go out and buy something? Why is it always my job to pay for the food, pick it up and serve it to you? What do you do around here? You are not handicapped; you can do something. This is it; I'm done allowing you to take advantage of me. I am tired. Either you get out or get a job. Better yet, you can just get out," Ivy yelled.

Ken was surprised at her reaction, especially since he had done her housework. "Slow down, where is this coming from?"

She walked into their office to avoid further argument. She noticed the receipt from the restaurant on her desk with the note from Chef. She was furious that he had gone through her pockets and wondered what he was looking for. She hoped he read the note and knew that another man found her attractive, and he needed to step up his game. When she came back into the living room to confront him about going through her pockets, someone knocked on the door before she could get started.

Ken thought one of the neighbors was knocking to complain about their loud arguing again. He flung open the door ready to start an argument with the neighbor. However, Ken was staring down the barrels of two guns pointing at his head.

The third officer handed him a search warrant. "Step out of the apartment, please. You are both being handcuffed and taken to the police car while we execute these search warrants. Please hand over your cell phones. Also, we need the passwords to your phones, laptop, tablets, and any other electronic equipment. If you don't release your passwords, we will find them anyway. Make it easy on yourselves."

Ken and Ivy complied. As they were being led to the police cars, Ivy started talking. She told the police that Ken spent all of his time on the computer. She gave them the information they needed about him being a computer expert and knowing how to do anything on the Internet. Ivy lied and said she didn't know what Ken did all day. She was singing like a bird. She flirted and tried to use her womanly charms so they wouldn't arrest her too. When the cops were out of the building, they handed Ivy over to a female officer who put her in the back of the police car. The female officer struck up a conversation with Ivy. She asked how Ivy got mixed up with Ken. Ivy told the story about him being fired from his stock market job.

As Ken was being taken to a different police car, the officers questioned him. He kept saying no comment and that he knew his rights. Legally, he didn't have to say anything, and he wanted a lawyer. He kept quiet in the police car.

The police found evidence of Grandma's information on the printer. Later at the police station, they uncovered files on the laptop, texts on the cell phone, and emails all of which put the nails in his coffin. Ivy's cell phone didn't have anything that would incriminate her.

Both were taken to the police station. Ken was arrested and booked on identity theft. When they questioned Ivy, she said she didn't know anything, and all of this was news to her. They asked her who supplied Ken with the data that was found on his laptop. Ivy lied and said she didn't know.

INVESTIGATIONS

The 5-Sir Company hired an investigator. He looked at all the cameras along the route and in the area where the truck stopped. He ordered the city's camera footage. There was nothing available. *This was an elaborately planned robbery.* There was one grainy picture from a city camera on top of the traffic light. He was not able to see what happened, but he did see Jacob on the ground. He was able to see 4 numbers on the license plate of the getaway truck. He called it in. It had been stolen from a job site about a week ago. They found it abandoned and whipped of fingerprints and hair. The investigator calculated the mileage from the robbery site to the truck termination site. It was about ten miles. Since this truck was so close to the border the agent figured they drove across the border in a waiting vehicle and disappeared in Canada. Just on a hunch, he calculated the miles from the robbery site to the city airport. It was exactly ten miles.

The investigator went to the airport. He asked the airport employee on duty for the flight log for Saturday afternoon and the camera footage of those entering and exiting the building and the tarmac. He saw the same truck pull into the yard and up to a plane. "Is it usual practice for an employee to escort a truck to a waiting plane??

"This is standard practice, especially if there is a timing issue and the plane must depart quickly. Since this is a private airport, we cater to our wealthy clientele with expensive planes."

"Who is the employee in the footage?"

"That is Mr. Oliver, he's a new employee, but a fast learner."

The personnel files revealed the address was a PO Box, and the phone number was the disconnected burner phone. They reviewed the footage again and zoomed in on Mr. Oliver, he was wearing a hat and glasses, and his face was not clear. It did not match the photo in his personnel file. The investigator went back to the video and zoomed in on the guys unloading the truck. All he could see was their backs as they got out of the truck and loaded everything onto the plane.

He asked to see the plane travel log. It indicated they are flying to Africa, but that airport was not zoned for international travel. The airport employee assumed it was an error and the correct location was Arizona.

"Was Mr. Oliver the only one working on Saturday afternoon?"

"No, there are usually two people working each shift, but this footage was during lunch, so he was the only one here at that time. He had to escort the truck because the other guy was at lunch. Usually, Mr. Oliver prefers to stay at the desk because he has a breathing problem. Sitting at a desk was perfect for him because he needed to use his inhaler a lot."

The investigator thanked him and went on his way. He reported all his findings to the 5-Sir Company. He told them that that vaccine in Africa was theirs and if they wanted him to go for more research, he would be willing to get to the bottom of it. The 5-Sir Company decided to keep it in-house and wrote the robbery off as a loss.

JACOB

It was discharge day for Jacob. Emily gathered Jacob's things from the hospital and put them in an overnight bag. She brought the car to the front so when he was discharged, he wouldn't have to wait. The children were scurrying around trying to be helpful. While waiting on the discharge papers and the prescriptions from the hospital pharmacy, Jacob checked his other account and saw that Drake did not wire the rest of his money. It was good because the 5-Sir investigator looked at his finances. Jacob explained the $10,000 was a loan from his friend so he could fix up the house.

The news flashed on Jacob's TV in the hospital. *"We have breaking news. We interrupt your regularly scheduled program with exciting news regarding South Sudan Africa. There has been an anonymous donation of the vaccine and the booster. It is a miracle. The people in Africa are no longer dying. Thank you, anonymous donor, whoever you are. We now return you to your regularly scheduled program."* Everyone was thinking the same thing, but no one said a word about the anonymous donor. This must be the vaccine that was stolen from Jacob.

The nurse came with a wheelchair. Kimberly wanted to push it, but the nurse explained it was part of her job, and that it was best for her patient. She pushed Jacob's wheelchair out to the curb where Emily was waiting in the car. The girls helped him out of the wheelchair; Cameron opened the car door and helped him get into the car. Jacob loved to hear the three of them in the back seat chopping it up. It was great to see them getting along. Kayla held on to her dad's medicine and discharge papers as if they were gold. All their energy and focus were on their dad. As the triplets chatted amongst themselves, Jacob and Emily were engaged in their conversation.

GRANDMA/GRANDKIDS

Grandma gathered the grandkids and solicited their help to make Roy's house spick-and-span. They complained about the smell but helped to make it livable and smell good.

Cameron rented a carpet shampooer. The girls had rubber gloves and threw out a lot of junk. They removed one of the sofas, a broken chair, and the broken end tables. Now there was a clear path through the house. She had no idea what to do with all of Roy's knee braces. They washed about ten loads of clothes. Grandma folded the clothes and put them in the dresser drawers. She scrubbed the bathroom from top to bottom. They must have used a half gallon of bleach.

Grandma also bought a few plants. Now Roy's place was suitable for recovery. She scheduled in-home physical therapy and in-home nurse visits. Like a good sister, she lived with Roy for three weeks until he could get around by himself with his walker. Afterward, she visited in the mornings. After two months, she was sure he was doing well and limited the visits to a couple of times a week. Grandma arranged the free senior transportation service to correspond with his doctor's appointments. Sometimes, she took him to the doctor's appointments to stay updated on his progress. She put First Sunday dinners on hold for a few months.

GRANDMA/KEN

Jacob took the day off work to take Grandma to Ken's trial. He promised not to confront anyone and to remain calm. Ken was sentenced to fifteen years in state prison for identity theft, five years for Cybercrimes, another five years for credit card fraud, and five more years in federal prison for tampering with the US mail, which was a federal offense.

Ivy was not in the courtroom. Earlier, she got off with five years of probation. After all, they couldn't prove her involvement because everything was on Ken's laptop. She was making plans to move in with the Chef.

Grandma asked the judge if she could ask Ken a question. He said yes.

"Why did you do this to me? Did you pick me out of the sky, or was I your target? Did I do something to hurt you?"

Ken answered, "Your daughter, Madison was my girlfriend for over five years."

"Oh, Ken now I remember you. You were a kind and considerate man who would call me every year on my birthday. I worked on your Mayoral campaign. I wondered what happen to you when you dropped out of politics. We were so proud of you. You were a young man from the city who worked his way almost to the top. Stocks and bonds were how you made your living. Baby, you broke Madison's heart. She cherished you and you betrayed her when you got married and still courting her. What happened that made you turn to a life of crime?"

"Yes, Ma'am it's me. I was wrong and got married while still dating her and juggled my wife and Madison for about two years. I was good at scheduling my time with each of them. Madison had no idea I was married until someone showed her pictures. Because I hurt her deeply, Madison destroyed my life when she lied and told my boss I took drugs and that I threatened to assault her. I lost my job as a Financial Analyst. My reputation was damaged, and no one would hire me. I lost my standing with the Stock Exchange. I was blacklisted in the financial district. I lost my home, money, and standing in the community. I became a shell of a man with no income and no ability to make money, all because of Madison. In all fairness, she did apologize for that lie, but I still could not get my job back. When she died, I was so angry. It brought back all of those feelings. The only way to calm my rage was to get revenge. Since she was dead, I could not get my revenge on her, so I used all my skills and resources and got my revenge on you and your grandson.

"What about my son? Did you shoot him?"

"No, that is not my style. The computer is my weapon of choice, not firearms."

The Judge stopped the exchange. "That's enough, get him out of here."

JACOB/DRAKE

Jacob passed the necessary security to visit Drake in jail. It was a place he never wanted to go. He walked past the round tables where the families were visiting. He was escorted to a corner table where Drake was waiting, alone. A guard was standing close with his hand on his gun.

"Hey man, how is it going in here?" Jacob asked.

"You know this is my third strike and I'm in here for life unless my attorney finds a loophole," Drake explained.

"Yes, I knew that. Sorry. What did they get you for?"

"It's the strangest thing. They got me for drug trafficking. I set up several drops in Detroit with customers I've done business with for years. I guess one turned me in."

"I believe that is called karma, my man."

"What do you mean?"

"For what you did to my sister. God has a way of turning everything around. I remembered what Madison told me. I made a few calls to the outer circle that you ignored, they were glad to spill the tea. Then I put two and two together which confirmed what you did. I had to tolerate your trifling butt and pretended I was down with you on everything so I could get close enough to fill in the gaps about your California operation so I could turn you in. Most of the validation was in those duffle bags you asked me to take from your hotel room. Man, you handed me everything I needed. Yes, I did it. You know that stop I had to make before going to work that Saturday morning; it was to the police. I gave them copies of everything in that bag. I told them about your entire operations in California.

Jacob took a breath and looked Drake in the eyes, "Yeah, Madison told me about the drug manufacturing, distribution, and smuggling. She also told me you had several locations - one mixed, one cooked, one cut, and multiple distribution locations. She said this process guaranteed you could not be caught with a product and the most significant benefit was that no one else knew how to produce your finished product. Yes, Madison knew it all. She told me. But man, she would have never told the police. Since you are time OCD, I knew the precise moment you would be back in your hotel after the job so they could make the arrest."

Jacob sat back in his chair looking very relaxed and continued, "The police told me they had surveillance on you in Detroit the day Madison died. They also told me that her car accident was not an accident. The brakes were tampered with. You know what, my ex-brother-in-law; the thing that broke, shattered then disintegrated my heart was they lifted many fingerprints from the brake pads, and one of them belonged to you. The police figured you bought some used and worn brake pads and had someone put them on her car."

With a heavy heart, Jacob continued. "You thought she would turn you in because she knew too much, so you had her killed. Madison, my only sister, is in the bitter cold grave, and you are in the freezing, cold, nasty cell block grave. That's what you get; I hope you rot in here."

Drake was surprised that Jacob would rat him out. "Jacob, how stupid do you think I am? I have attorneys who will plead my case and I just might beat the rap. Don't forget, I am well connected inside and outside of this prison. You have not seen the last of me. I can bring you down too."

"Man, you made sure we covered our steps very well with the vaccine job. All of the phones are at the bottom of the lake; the money can't be traced to me. All of the cameras were disabled, and my face is not on anything. Bring me down? I wish you would. Connected? Please. I am connected, locked, and loaded. If anything happens to me or anyone in my family, the contract I have on you will be enforced."

"Watch your back, my brother. This is not over!"

Jacob smiled, stood up, and said "Duces." He flashed the peace sign across his chest and walked out. Jacob did not look back. The shock on Drake's face gave him satisfaction and revenge for Madison's death, which brought peace to his mind, body, and soul.

As Jacob drove off the lot, the radio interrupted the music with a news flash. *We interrupt your program for a special news break. This just in... here is an update regarding the people in Africa who received the vaccine from an anonymous donor. It has been administered and there have been zero deaths in the last 48 hours. It is a miracle. No one can explain where it came from. We think it was from the 5-Sir company's robbery, but this cannot be verified. There is no comment from the 5-Sir company. The good news is the people are not dying. Everyone let's celebrate life. We now return you to your program.*

Jacob smiled as he continued to drive off the prison lot. God had a way of turning bad into good. Jacob took a moment and thanked God. He pulled his car into a shopping mall lot and began to pray:

Dear God, Drake is the worst of the worst.

I know I did not do the right thing by helping him steal the vaccine.

Please forgive me for not being honest with my

family or the 5-Sir company.

Thank you for allowing me to get away and not get caught.

Thank you for allowing me to keep my job.

And God, I really, really appreciate you sparing my life.

We did a good thing for the people in

Motherland but in the wrong way.

Thank you for getting the vaccine to the people in Africa.

Jacob's phone rang and he ended his prayer.

"Hi Dad, are you busy?" his daughter inquired.

"No Kayla, I'm driving home. What's on your mind?"

"Dad, I have something to tell you. I know you will be mad at me, but I have to express my truth. It is burning a hole in my heart, and I must let it out. You won't love me after I tell you," Kayla whispered.

"That is not true! I'm your father. I will love you no matter what you tell me. You know you can talk to me about anything, right? Go ahead baby girl; tell me what's on your heart that is troubling you so much. I am here and I'm listening."

GRANDMA

She heard the news about the people in Africa doing better. Grandma called Roy: "Did you hear the news about the folks in Africa?"

"Yes, Sis. It is a beautiful thing."

"I'm just checking on you dear brother, take care of yourself and I will see you tomorrow."

She was feeling very grateful for everything.

"Dear Heavenly Father,

I thank you for this anonymous person who

donated the vaccine to your people in Africa.

In my spirit, I feel these are the people

who shot and robbed my son.

I forgive them.

God, I thank you that they did not kill my child.

I don't understand why this had to happen,

but I know we are stronger because of it.

Thank you for all the wonderful things you have given us.

It is still a beautiful world, full of wonders and surprises.

I pray for the entire world,

I pray that sickness and disease are eliminated.

I pray that people will not be selfish with knowledge or cures.

I pray that healing will sweep over the world faster than any
sickness ever can.
I pray that holistic and pharmaceutical
resources unite and become the norm.

I pray that everyone will see and understand
that it is your mighty hand working to cure all diseases.
And Dear God, I pray for peace.
Not just peace from wars,
I pray for peace within every person's heart and soul.
I pray that this hate that was planted and grew like a weed
will be poisoned and destroyed with love.
I pray that hate will shrivel up and die.
I pray that gun violence will stop
and we lean on you to calm the rage
and talk instead of shoot
Lord, we need a law to mandate that people take a conflict
resolution class
before purchasing a gun.
Dear God, I pray that as we go to church, school,
or any gathering, we can do so without
worrying about an active shooter.
Give us back the confidence and assurance of safety.
God, please move in a mighty way.
Dear Lord, please cover us with your grace and mercy.
I pray that we have individual and corporate peace
in the middle of a storm.
Lord hide us in the eye of the storm and no harm comes to us.

I know it rains on the good as well as the bad.
I ask that you envelop us in love
so when bad times come, we will draw upon your strength
and will face any colossal situation
because it will be you within us.
And last but not least, My Father,
I pray that you forgive us for the
wrongs we've committed knowing and not knowing.
In your son Jesus' name. Amen.

The end.

Thank you for reading my book. I appreciate you! I would be very honored if you would submit a review on Amazon.com

If you are interested in my future projects, please feel free to send an email. PublishingStrong@gmail.com

Keep in touch:

Email:PublishingStrong@gmail.com

Facebook:@PublishingStrong

Instagram:@PublishingStrong

Twitter:@PublishingStron

Pinterest:www.Pinterest.com/PublishingStrong

LinkedIn:www.linkedin.com/in/marilyn-strong-ab1671159

YouTube:bit.ly/34XvJJe

Snail MailPublishing Strong

18640 Mack Avenue, # 413

Grosse Pointe Woods, MI 48236

9 781735 604831